A PATRIOT DIRGE

A JAZZMAN NOVEL

BY JACK RANDOM

CROW DOG PRESS
TURLOCK CA USA

A Patriot Dirge

A Jazzman Novel

By Jack Random

Published by
Crow Dog Press
1241 Windsor Court
Turlock CA 95380

Cover photograph by David Short, Windsor UK, 18 December 2011: The Day Vaclav Havel Died.

ISBN-13: 978-0692548196
ISBN-10: 069254819X

A PATRIOT DIRGE

To my wife
Julie Marie Bradford
For her patience and understanding

NOVEMBER 2015

A Patriot Dirge
The Cause and The Cost

In life he did not know him. In death, he admired him and mourned his passing. The more he learned, the greater his understanding of humanity's loss. He was the kind of man he would have liked to bring into this too often cold and unforgiving world. He knew what he believed and he chose to act on his convictions.

By every value we embrace, by every standard we bring to bear as citizens of a civilized, democratic world, Daniel Volcek was a hero and a patriot. Not because he recognized the inherent virtue of authority but because he defied it. Not because he believed in the sanctity of the law and obeyed but because he recognized a greater moral code and refused to allow the law to stand in the way of justice.

Daniel gave his life not willingly but knowingly. He knew the risk but he did not want to die. He did not wish to become a martyr. He saw what needed to be done and he acted. Random chance and circumstance took his life and made him a hero to thousands upon thousands who believed as he did.

Throughout our history our brightest patriots have

almost always come from outside the established order: Thomas Paine, Mahatma Gandhi, Martin Luther King, George Washington Carver, Howard Zinn, Jean-Paul Sartre, Simone de Beauvoir, Vaclav Havel. It requires no courage to uphold authority for its own sake. It takes courage to stand on the other side of the divide when the boots begin to march, the batons begin to fall, and the blood of injustice spills on the streets.

Now, the young man's inert body, contained in a plain black coffin, followed the same steps that the Czech Republic's playwright president once traveled on his last tour of his beloved Prague. Rome marched behind the coffin, carried by eight of his colleagues in the familiar masks of Guy Fawkes, and behind the New Orleans style band playing the tearful mourning jazz that the dead man once loved. Rome marched on, one step preceding the next, letting the waves of sorrow, the ocean of tears, wash over him.

Our ends never know our means or the price they carry. If we knew in the beginning, would we choose the same path? Would we compromise? Would we play it safe? There would be time for reflection. This was not that time. This was a time for mourning.

As he reached his destiny, his burial plot at Vinohrady cemetery, the band broke into the up tempo phase of the dirge. It meant that those he knew and those who knew him, those he loved and those who loved him, should celebrate his life and leave his death behind in the cold fertile ground of his final resting place.

Swiping tears from his face, Rome wondered if that was possible. The time for reflection was upon him. He felt the darkness seize his soul and he hoped it would not paralyze him as it had so often in the past, as it had in fact when this great adventure began so many years ago.

PART I

THE INDEPENDENCE MOVEMENT

JANUARY 2005

BILLIE SINGS THE BLUES

Tapping the Lower Depths

Who is poisoning the soul of America?

Patriotism. The Patriot Act. Drums of a march in protest. Red stains on a concrete wall. Clenched fists of rage. Cries of Treason! The sting of police batons on battered flesh. The smell of tear gas. Blood streaked eyes. Dark skinned people in army fatigues. Mercenary soldiers. Contract players. Red, white and greed.

Billie Holiday sings the blues.

Hell is a place of fury. Dante's Inferno. City of shadows, broken and scattered. Cries of a child. The smell of burning flesh. Tears of a mother. Shouts of rage. A people divided against itself, against its tormenters, against its captors, against its oppressors, against its liberators, against the invaders, against the curse of an angry god.

Do soldiers of god wear uniforms?

Does Jesus wave a flag?

The new patriots declare war on dissent, war on privacy, war on civil liberties, war on justice, war on activism, war on free speech, war on clean air and water, war on alternative energies, war on peace, war on journalism, war on labor, and war on democracy itself.

Billie Holiday sings the blues.

From the porch of his cabin overlooking Puget Sound, Rome was in mourning. He had given his all to defeating George W. Bush in the 2004 election. Now, alone with his thoughts, he confronted the demons of failure.

What was the point of political engagement when money and those who possessed mass quantities of it governed the process? What good did it do to speak out when a single voice had no chance of breaking through a cacophony of voices? The rightwing ideologues and demagogues set the agenda and the rest of us only fed the machine.

His entry into the world of politics was driven by a deeply rooted conviction, inherited from his radical upbringing, that the next great revolution in American democracy was the fall of the two-party system. He wrote incessantly, publishing a series of manifestos on the web, gathering people of like mind hungry for battle and willing to sacrifice.

In an age of growing unrest and governmental indifference to the working class and outright antagonism of the poor, he was convinced that the Independence Movement was poised to break through the general malaise, poised to challenge and shake the stranglehold of two parties under a common, corporate flag.

All that was before September 11, 2001, the day that changed everything.

Looking back, he recognized the inevitability of the chain of events that followed. They took the lead in the antiwar movement, opposing the invasion of Afghanistan. However backward and inhumane the

Taliban was, they were not responsible for the attack on this nation. They had inherited al Qaeda from the CIA, which had recruited, supplied and financed the terrorist group in its war against the Soviet Union.

In the days before the invasion, the Taliban had offered to turn Osama bin Laden and the al Qaeda leadership over to a third country to face charges before an international tribunal. Our government dismissed the offer out of hand. We were determined to offer the world a display of American power. These were among the many facts lost in the mythology of modern American history.

When we announced to the world the Bush Doctrine of preemptive strike and perpetual military superiority and turned our attention to Saddam Hussein, it became clear that our government was determined to create an enemy that would define our foreign policy for generations to come.

Saddam Hussein was only one in a long line of American supported tyrants, a line that included such luminous characters as Pinochet, Suharto, Pol Pot, Noriega, Musharraf and the Shah of Iran. The only connection Saddam shared with Osama bin Laden and al Qaeda was that both were well connected with the American intelligence community.

The war quickly became the all-encompassing issue. The Independence Movement was on hold, channeling all its resources and efforts to the antiwar movement. There were days of glory, days when it seemed the war machine could be stopped, and days when momentum gathered like a rising storm, sweeping across the nation and the world. There were days of rising hope as millions took to the streets in protest and the world community stood as one against the new American imperialism.

Howard Dean took the lead in the Democratic primaries. He became the focal point, the rallying cry, and the unifying voice of political opposition. The antiwar movement resisted the initial impulse to endorse a Democrat, fearing that they were being swept into a process that would inevitably yield to corruption.

They were disturbed by Dean's unqualified support of the Gulf War, the invasion of Afghanistan, and his ambivalence toward former President Bill Clinton who had only served to advance the forces of militarism and corporate dominance that were now in complete control of government.

Ultimately, it was the attack of other Democrats and the party, itself, that convinced Rome and his circle to support the Dean candidacy. He at least had the appearance of independence and held forth the greatest chance of success.

He cursed himself for not foreseeing what the Bush people had in mind. They handed over titular sovereignty to the Iraqi people in July and began a measured withdrawal of troops in August. They gambled that Iraq would not descend into anarchy and civil war before the election and won. They neutralized the antiwar movement.

What did it matter? What could he have done? A man without a platform is a man without a voice.

As it turned out, the Democratic nominee was irrelevant. The October surprise should not have surprised anyone. The public appeal of Osama bin Laden, himself, the duplicity of the Democratic candidate, and a Republican electoral fraud machine sealed a razor thin victory.

A PATRIOT DIRGE

No candidate could have defeated George W. Bush in 2004. Only the truth could have altered the course of history and no one was on the job.

What was the truth?

Karl Rove and the Bush administration used gay marriage, abortion and election fraud in order to win a second term they could not have won on their record of incompetence and deception. They were masters of propaganda, manipulators of fear and false patriotism. They fooled the people when it counted most with tax breaks weighted to the richest of Americans, with promises of security and moral values founded in Christian fundamentalism.

What would Jesus think of robbing the poor, the infirm and working people to feed the coffers of international corporations and send the indoctrinated off to war?

We had to give credit to the Bush political machine. They had masterfully orchestrated the reelection campaign. They had fooled most of the people most of the time. Their hold on power was never seriously threatened.

Now they could proceed without political constraint. They would reenter Iraq with a stone cold vengeance. They would rely on mercenary soldiers until another attack convinced a fear struck electorate that conscription was necessary. They would expand the war to Syria and Iran. They would launch a preemptive attack on North Korea using tactical nuclear weapons. They would intensify covert operations in Venezuela, Brazil, Guatemala, Mexico and anywhere else that "free trade" was threatened. They would push the war on terrorism to such lengths that no succeeding president, regardless of party, would even consider the option of retreat.

This was the vision that Rome saw every night as he closed his eyes to the waking world. It was the reason he no longer slept. He was little more than a walking corpse, a pale shadow of himself, and he yearned to be set free.

Billie Holiday sings the blues. A song of suicide: Strange Fruit.

He could feel the fall, like a rush of cold wind pulling at his brain, and he knew it was different from anything he had gone through before. This time he would go beyond the depths of his own destruction. This time he would not resist.

He moved from the city to his cabin on the Sound, a secluded location overlooking the ragged cliffs of the northern Pacific. This was where he felt alive. This was where he had discovered his true spirit. This was where he heard the cry of the forbearers and the call to arms. It was the place that fed his soul and healed his wounds. If the salty air and majestic vision of the Sound could not breathe him back to life, there was no more to live.

He knew from the unbreakable cycles of his life, it would be a long road. It was as it had always been. Every visit to the hole went deeper than the one preceding it. It was the golden rule that was as much a part of him as hope: He would descend ever deeper into the darkness before he could return to light. He would come to hate everyone and everything he valued. He would turn that hatred against himself and, if he survived, he would emerge from the hole a man reborn with newly discovered purpose.

It was not the way of his choosing but it was the way of his life. It was not as it should be; it was as it was. It was the way god or whatever entity goes beyond our control laid out for him.

As the plaintive calm, the majesty and beatitude of the northern Pacific began to grow cold with the first signs of fall and then winter, Rome was inhaling smoke and flame. His anger pierced the heart of sorrow, destroying all things beautiful and endearing. He let the darkness in. He invited it. He opened his chest and summoned every wayward spirit, every demon, ghost and malevolence within his realm, like an innocent invites a vampire into his home.

Rome was alone with his poisoned thoughts and struggling to find a way out. He did what he always did when he found himself sinking deep into the void. He pulled out his old, battered saxophone and played.

Then he began to write.

Billie Holiday sang the blues.

He could not give up now. The movement was still alive. They were bruised and battered, ripped and scattered, but they were still there. The despondence and humiliation would pass and the rage would inevitably breathe new life into the spirit of opposition. The loss of purpose and despair could be channeled into the outrage of renewed activism. The war was not over. It was only beginning.

Billie Holiday sang the blues. What choice did she have? It was what she was meant to do, what she had to do, what the gods demanded. Billie sang the blues and Rome Mason sang with her.

He found his voice and the words poured out in a river of rage, dancing on the edge of despair until they found their way home. Jazz.

THE PROPAGANDIST

Finding a Voice
Resisting the Call

Roy was a writer without a voice.

For decades he had toiled in the trade of all scribes, searching for a form, a platform, a format that would suit his talent and sensibilities. He wrote plays, random poetry, short stories, and even managed to publish a novel under the banner of an Emerging Voice. In his mid forties with rapidly graying hair, he found it difficult to look in the mirror and witness an emerging voice. The image that gazed back at him was a man without one. He possessed passion, boundless curiosity, a command of language, and an unwavering desire to communicate his vision of the world, but no voice.

When he looked behind him, he saw a pattern of failure: failed relationships, a faltering career as a high school English teacher, and most damning of all, a failure to cultivate his creative potential. He had been a writer from the moment he first put pencil to paper. At the age of eight, he wrote his own epitaph, a message to the world in the event of his sudden death: A testament to his youthful philosophy, founded on principles of justice, equal rights and the quest for harmony in a divisive world, he carried the document in the back pocket of his jeans for the better part of a year – an eternity in the life of a child.

His writing voice was as natural as his speaking voice yet in his desire for success, he fell victim to the academic demigods of the written form. He read writers on writing, attended writers conferences and attempted to adapt the formulaic methods of publishable writing. He cursed them now for wasting so many years and warping his creative impulse.

Who were they anyway but writers trying to transform momentary success into a steady income? What sense did it make to erect barriers based on rules that would fall as soon as the academic overlords decided on a new school of thought?

Their prohibitions on adverbs, adjectives and passive sentence structures were counterintuitive to the creative process. Open a work by Gabriel Garcia Marquez at random and count the adjectives, adverbs and passive verb phrases. Whom would you rather adopt as a model of writing: Gabriel Garcia Marquez, a master of contemporary literature whose work will live as long as the printed word, or Robert Olin Butler, a Pulitzer Prize winning author who quickly faded into academic obscurity, subject to the familiar summation: First work, best work?

Their obsession with the senses and finding your one true voice were distractions that did little but obstruct the natural flow of words and thoughts. They were artificial impositions that enabled academicians to pronounce a work worthy or unworthy but they only branded contemporary literature with a distortion peculiar to the times. When an internal editor is in place before the first word is committed to paper, the cause is lost.

He tried to play by the rules but he could not honor them. Failure followed failure until failure became the motif. He turned against himself and everyone around him, friends, family and colleagues bore the brunt of his disease.

His family had not so much abandoned him as he abandoned them. He could no longer bear to scrutinize his failure through their eyes. He could no longer listen to their words of encouragement, their testimonials of faith, their whispered disparagement, their knowing glances. There came a time when could smell the mendacity over the scent of honeyed ham and tri-tip lathered in A1 steak sauce at family barbecues and holiday gatherings.

He surrendered a faltering relationship, quit his job and moved to San Carlos, close enough to San Francisco to hang and far enough to pay the rent. He found a job stacking books at City Lights on Columbus Avenue, birthplace of the beats, center of free speech in the city of tolerance, and began to write as if every word was a down payment on his life, his soul, and his place on a dying planet.

When the nation went to war, first in Afghanistan and then in Iraq, his voice found him. It was not the voice of a poet or a novelist; it was the voice of a propagandist. He appealed to the heart as well as the mind, striking the chords of passion and outrage, moving his readers to righteous indignation and leaving them hungry for a course of action. He provided slogans, banners and rationales for a growing movement in opposition to war.

Like any self-respecting propagandist in modern

politics, he assumed a name and soon found his commentaries pulsing through the internet, the alternative media, gathering their own momentum, knocking down doors of perception, scratching at the chalkboards of the intellectual elite, crashing through ideological barriers and partisan divides, finding a home at the heart of radical political discourse.

He could breathe again. He could hear the song of the seagulls and the pounding waves. He could taste the promise of rebirth in an ocean mist. He could feel the pulse of god's blue green earth and he embraced it.

He attended political events, discussion forums, speeches, rallies, and joined the exploding march of protest in the streets.

He took walks along the embarcadero, smiled at strangers and rediscovered a lost sense of hope in the setting sun. He enjoyed life again and the chore of living it was a small price to pay. Amidst a crumbling world, ravaged by war and toxic neglect, he lived in a place of contentment.

And in that place, on the west coast of the left bank, in an enclave sheltered from the storm, he received an invitation that would threaten once again to alter his destiny and turn his reality inside out.

When a man has struggled so desperately so long to find a place where peace is as natural as awakening, it is difficult to take another step. He let it rest and quietly went on with his life, hoping that it would fade like a distant memory.

It did not. It gnawed at his gut like an internal gash. It played with his mind and distracted his thoughts. It shadowed him like a partner once betrayed. It stole the taste of fine wine, soured the joy of breathing and gave the ocean breeze a haggard bite.

The ironies of life are rich with opportunities and fraught with danger. In the context of his philosophy, the risk was always worth taking but he was determined now to follow a path where heart and mind came together in harmony.

THE ACTIVIST

Amy's Choice
Loving the Cause
Hating the Call

Roy was a self-proclaimed second rate Tom Paine. He gave himself to the cause but confined his activities primarily to writing. He was a writer, not a soldier, not an activist, not an organizer or operative. He found comfort in his role as a propagandist for the movement. A man of letters is not supposed to risk his all as Paine did when he marched with the Continental Army in the early days of the War for Independence. Even Paine would learn: Survival was his duty and writing was his call.

Amy was a vital member of a growing resistance movement. She was an activist, not a weekend protester. She was a gutter to the penthouse activist, a grassroots organizer, a rabble-rouser and pamphleteer, recruiter and strategist.

She engaged in civil disobedience, broke windows, chained herself to buildings and splattered red paint on the persons and properties of corporate mercenaries. She had been tried, beaten and jailed for the cause. When the cops formed lines of oppression, Amy was on the front lines of resistance and she never broke rank. If Roy was a part of the cause, Amy was its heart.

The concept of an old soul is reserved for those whose depth and breadth of knowledge cannot be explained by education and experience. If there is such a thing, Amy was an old soul. She consumed knowledge as if it was manna, from the ancient philosophers to contemporary politics, and transformed it into a vision that engaged and pulled at the essence of humanity.

When Amy invited Roy to a meeting of minds, he did not think twice. She was always recruiting, always cajoling, appealing, and building the movement. He was a man who contributed modestly to the cause; he was not the sort to attract anything more than intellectual curiosity in a woman of her stature. He figured he was one of dozens, maybe more, to be invited to this gathering.

He was wrong. It was a small gathering. No more than nine or ten people of like mind, all committed to the cause. Most of the evening was spent in groups of two or three, talking about the issues of the day, sharing observations as spectators on the planet. The conversation was free and flowing. Nothing was off limits. Not even the self-imposed censorship – the internal editors that calculate a probable impact before a remark is delivered – seemed to be operative.

A man who was never quite comfortable in the company of others, Roy was more relaxed and self-assured than he had ever been.

As the evening edged to its conclusion, Roy found himself sitting under a starlit sky with a woman he both admired and desired: Amy.

Until now, he wondered if she was avoiding him.

He felt his spirit rise as she approached. He took pleasure in the sound of her voice, infused with passion and curiosity, a voice of free jazz that held him captive and stimulated wonder. More than anything, he wondered why she had saved the endpoint of a pleasant evening for him.

The tone became more pressing and dark when she told him about a man who had given his life for the cause. She emphasized that he gave it willingly, that when the time came, he did not hesitate.

They had worked together at a halfway house, a place where dissidents throughout the world could escape the oppression of their governments. The work brought them into conflict with numerous international intelligence agencies. An agent from Interpol got too close to the operation and Gerard took it upon himself to become an informant. When he turned out to be a misinformant, he was renditioned to an unknown location. Six months later, his body turned up in Saudi Arabia as a victim of a terrorist attack.

Roy began to realize there was more to this encounter than a budding romance or intellectual pursuit. Was it possible Amy was an undercover agent? Was it a setup? He had been told that activists had been recruited to the government's cause. The traitors were often leaders with passionate voices. He looked into her dark brown eyes and recoiled at the thought. If anyone was pure and incorruptible, it was Amy.

Still, it was becoming clear that she was asking him to go beyond his comfort. He was only a writer, a propagandist, a craftsman of words to arouse the heart and soul. He promoted the cause from a distance. His dissidence carried some element of risk but only within definable limits. He had no desire to become a martyr.

Had she misjudged him?

She explained in a rush that there was an opening in the organization and that every member needed a match. Couples did not meet the government profile of an enemy of state. She explained that Roy was her match. He was chosen and would have only two chances to decline. If he did not accept, it was understood he would never see Amy or her friends again – at least not as acquaintances.

He saw his own internal struggle in her face. She appreciated his dilemma. It was not a decision to be taken lightly. Had it not been Amy, he would not have given it second thought.

He was not a martyr, not a hero; he was a writer, a propagandist, a man of words. He knew his role and accepted it. Amy understood his integrity. He would not join a cause for a woman. He was too old for tales of romance. He would not join any cause for anyone or anything except the cause itself. It was why he was chosen. Neither Amy nor Roy nor any of Amy's comrades would be content with anything less than total commitment.

"I'll have to think about it long and hard," he finally said.

There was relief in her eyes, which he interpreted as a protective instinct. She allowed her hand to rest upon his before she rose to join the others in a large circle around a fire. He realized that they were all committed, all paired. Only Amy remained alone.

Roy went home and obsessed. He had turned her down once and with her a life he could only imagine, a life of certain adventure and challenge. He did not know whether he could turn her down again. He did not know whether in fact, he would have a second chance but he was grateful she had held out that promise.

He would not hear from her again for seven months.

EMERGING FROM THE VOID

Riding the Dragon
Toward the Light

It had been seven months since Rome had retired to the cabin. The floors, tables and chairs were strewn with books, articles, newspapers and notes. Notes everywhere. He rode the dragon through layers of introspection and extrospection. He examined his psyche and his place in the world. He punished himself for his failings and remembered his virtues. He had relived his life from the womb to the sunrise that now graced the northern Pacific on a clear June morn.

The dragon was crashing. He was emerging from the darkness and moving steadily toward the light.

It was time to clean house. It was time to clear out all the old ideas, the archives of past struggles, to make room for the new. It was time to organize his thoughts, formulate his plans and renew his contacts.

Only the goals remained: Stop the war, end the occupation, redefine foreign policy, defend civil liberties and build an independent movement to challenge the dominance of corporate politics.

The questions that remained were: How far was he willing to go? Would he compromise one objective (as he had done in 2004) to achieve another? Did his priorities reflect his values? Could the resistance find a formula that would hold them together?

No matter how much things seemed to change, these were very much the same questions that dissidents had always faced. Progressive movements rarely achieved lasting unity. When they did, it was invariably the result of some cataclysmic event like the Great Depression or the Vietnam War.

The traditional wedge issues in Republican politics were as potent as ever and now they added fear of a terrorist attack. Was opposition to the Iraq War powerful enough to overcome the coalition of rightwing neocons and Christian fundamentalists?

Was he ready for the struggle ahead? Was he ready to meet the world? In an age of technological acceleration, would the world he greeted, after a prolonged absence, be the same world he left behind? He was completely cut off. Every bit of news and analysis he possessed was at least seven months old. Anything could have happened: an assassination, another terrorist attack, civil unrest, martial law or an environmental catastrophe.

He was suddenly hungry for the same sources of news and information he had cast out of his life in order to discover or rediscover his soul.

As soon as he put his house in order, he began to plan his reentry into society: a drive to Vancouver, a ferry to Port Townsend and then Seattle.

He did not hurry the journey; he took time to talk to the people who lived and worked in the world. In coffee houses and bars, he sat quietly, opened his mind and listened as he had never listened before.

He listened to Canadian lumberjacks, tired of a

corrupt Liberal government, hoping that better relations with the Americans would somehow translate into a better life for themselves and their families. He listened to angry leftists, railing on Canadian cooperation with American wars and neo-liberal trade policies. He listened to American waiters, retail workers, laid off industrial workers, workers of every trade, complaining about the decline of living standards, lost health benefits, collapsing pensions, declining wages, feckless unions, the cost of living and war. He listened to artists, writers, sculptors, musicians and designers wondering if they had lost their way – if there even was a place for them in the new world of global enterprise and manufactured consent.

By the time he crossed the Sound from Port Townsend to Seattle, he understood that people everywhere were undergoing the same period of doubt and reflection that had consumed him for seven months.

There was a change in the air. There was deep discontent. The people were looking for a way out of the void. They were still bogged down by the hunt for scapegoats and easy solutions but there was hope they would soon go beyond the standard automatic reactions. Deep down, every man and woman knew that human sexuality and the tragic necessity of abortion were not at the core of our problems. Every woman and man understood that religious values, like pharmaceutical drugs, were not solutions but only remedies to relieve the symptoms of disease.

Rome understood that the war, itself, was part of a much bigger problem and that it could not be isolated from the whole. The plight of the workingman was the plight of the Afghan, the plight of the Iraqi, the plight of the Paris suburbs, the plight of the Chinese industrial worker, the plight of the Guatemalan coffee farmer, and the plight of the woman behind the counter at Starbucks.

It came down to economics. It was not enough to stop a war when the powers behind the war would only start another. It was not enough to target any particular problem, no matter how global or earth changing, when the infrastructure of corporate control remained intact. Any solution to a global disease had to attack the root and source of the disease.

"I know you," said a woman with dark probing eyes.

Rome was sitting outdoors at a waterfront café, sipping a latte and devouring the *Times*, when a woman approached him without warning.

"You're Rome Mason," she said.

She sat down and they began to talk as if they were old friends. She knew him from his activism before the last election. She was aware of his sudden withdrawal from the movement. As they talked, Rome began to suspect that in the archives of things forgotten, he knew of her work as well.

"I didn't catch your name," he said.

"Amy," she replied. Just Amy.

This was not a chance meeting. She was holding something back. Something was building and she wanted Rome to be a part of it.

"We've been waiting for you," she said, as if reading his mind.

He smiled. It was good to know someone was waiting for him. She smelled of jasmine. Why hadn't he noticed before? It was the same scent Maggie had worn before the darkness pulled them apart. He had no sense of romance. She was much too young and his desire was all but spent. Dreams. Only dreams. Still, it was soothing to remember.

"We've been waiting for you to come out of retirement," she continued. "We knew the minute you hit Vancouver, you were back."

He did not wonder why or how. He knew there were ways to track a man. He had not tried to cover his tracks. He believed in fate. He believed there was a reason for every action, every thought and movement, every fluctuation of energy in the field of play. This was the reason he emerged from his hole. Amy was his connection to the world.

They shook hands and set a date for a meeting of minds. All the players would be in attendance.

THE HAMMER OF FATE

Fighting a Hurricane
Love and Free Choice

She called from Seattle. She had taken an apartment. In her occupation, moving was a frequent necessity. She wanted Roy to join her. He did not hesitate to agree.

When he arrived at the airport, he expected Amy to greet him. Instead, he found a man bearing his writing pseudonym. A dark skinned man with glimmering black hair a little longer than fashion, he introduced himself as Ravi and explained that Amy had been detained. He smiled when Roy's face registered alarm.

"Not that kind of detention," Ravi said.

They drove to a neighborhood in the University area where Ravi gave him a quick tour of a modern, spacious and tastefully done apartment. It had a woman's feel to it with the presence of a man – not what Roy expected. He was shown to the guest room, relatively sparse with a large bookshelf, desk and a framed photograph of Bob Dylan, Michael McClure and Allen Ginsberg circa 1965. The accommodations were not what concerned him, however. He was here because he could not deny a burning desire to see Amy at least one more time.

He fell asleep, dreaming of a maze of gray, stone alleys where Amy appeared and disappeared in lighted windows and darkened doorways, awakening some time later to the smell of roast beef. He shook the webs from his vision and descended the stairs, where he found a man and a woman sitting down to dinner. They introduced themselves as Fagin and Karin, the couple in residence and his hosts.

The mystery grew. Where was Amy? What was her role in this equation? Was this where she lived or only a shill?

They shared a meal over wine and delicate conversation. There was little they could tell him except that it was not a hard life. The risks were there but they were not a constant presence. They were allowed to live their lives for the most part pursuing whatever their dreams entailed. Fagin was a musician and poet while Karin was a photographer and performance artist.

Roy excused himself and went for a long walk along the tree-shaded streets of two-story townhouses and apartment buildings. He sat on a park bench to breathe the cool evening air and watch the birds, gophers and squirrels go about their business. There was little question in their little lives. A squirrel did not choose between nuts. It consumed them. A crow did not wander the highways looking for Don Juan. It went where the weather was warm and the food plentiful. It was only the human life form that extracted such drama from daily existence.

He thought about Amy and wondered why she chose to withhold her presence. Was it the equivalent of a bribe? If he did not go along with their plans, would he ever see her again? He was startled at how that thought suddenly ached.

He became aware of being observed. Looking across the parkway, he caught the eye of a large man with a full beard who tipped his cap. Soon he was surrounded by a group of men, none of whom were familiar yet he was not alarmed. He understood that this was his welcoming committee. He understood they were Amy's Seattle comrades. He was here to win their approval.

A stout bearded man with a thick neck, shaggy hair and a lumberjack hat wanted to know where he stood. Roy understood the question but he did not know how to answer. He remained uncertain, stymied by conflicting emotions. The man, one boot on the park bench, lit up his pipe and proclaimed with a good-natured chuckle: "Well, I guess Amy's going a bit cheap these days."

Roy felt the temperature in his face rise. If it was meant to stir his passion, it worked. He felt as if he was on trial. If he was unwilling or unable to defend the honor of a woman and a comrade, he was not worthy of admittance into their exclusive club.

"Well, then," he replied, not allowing another thought, "I accept."

They looked around before one of them, an imposing black man with heavy eyes, asked:

"You accept what?"

"Amy," he replied.

The mood instantly shifted to celebration, hand grasps and back slaps. Roy was in and Amy had a match. It was as if the entire event was choreographed. They piled into an old Dodge van and drove to a corner pub where Amy and the other women were waiting.

As if on cue, a pair of fiddlers played a crisp jig, the patrons clapped along, and a bright-eyed woman sang.

"You came around," said Amy smiling.

They embraced and Roy surrendered all misgivings. Amy was the core and center of his being now. She would become his mentor, protector and confidant. He gave her his faith on the code of honor, asking only for the warmth of her embrace in return.

Within hours, they were coupled in a ceremony born of heathen traditions. Two circles were formed, the outer moving clockwise, the inner counter clockwise, while Amy and Roy were thrust into the center. There they gave their oath, their pledge of loyalty beneath the glowing light of a harvest moon.

The party moved to the home of their hosts where the mood gradually became more subdued. Amy and Roy excused themselves and went upstairs to anoint their newborn union in the fountains of desire.

It was a dream. It was a dream more beautiful than anything he had encountered on this dull earth. It was a moment of paradise, a moment so pure it remains in the spirit eternal, crystallized in the psyche, beyond life itself. One can no more describe the unity of flesh than one can a unity of spirit, except by their signs and symptoms. When consciousness no longer distinguishes spirit from flesh, when the dance of dreams finds comfort within the body, when self is no longer apart from other, then the moans and natural lotions and scents and sweet salt tastes of love are marked by eternal bliss. Heaven on earth. Faith for nonbelievers. Prayers of the devout. Amy and Roy.

The mythical monk atop the mountain was right: You cannot find love; love can only find you.

THE DYING MAN

The Tyranny of Time
A Man without Restraint
Darkness and Light

In old age, John Sinclair discovered the tyranny of time. It was measured by the heartbeat of death, the relentless rites of passage, a long night's journey of endless mourning and the sorrow of being alone.

It was more than being alone in the literal sense. It was more than the absence of a life partner. That was as much a lifestyle choice as the cruel fate of chance. It was more than being abandoned by a family that did not share his values, his thirst for knowledge and his ambition. That too was a choice. One did not have to be lonely being alone.

It was rather the sense of being isolated from the world at large, from the society that molded his mental landscape, that inspired him to engage it on his own terms, and that left him in his twilight years utterly indifferent.

Sinclair was a dying man. It was not a medical diagnosis. To his knowledge, the only crippling disease he had was life itself. Still, he was dying. He felt it – the decay, the rust, the disintegration – in every movement of his aging body, in every thought and perception. It crept into his bones and shadowed him for a decade. In time, he came to welcome it as a blessing that freed him from the normal restraints of living.

Before death became his constant companion, Sinclair was a maker and breaker of kings, princes and the power brokers that pulled their strings behind the curtains of American politics. With death on his shoulder, he realized that everything he had accomplished in his career as a politic operative, everything for which he had been well compensated, was destructive of everything he believed.

With death as his brother, he had no need to please the eternal other. He had no need to appease the demons that curse lesser men. The dying man is above reproach. He is the ultimate weapon of good and evil. His only master is time and time is a cruel master.

There are times in a man's life - any man or any woman - when he could do almost anything - rape, murder, things too horrible to pull from the pit of unconscious thought - in order to realize his desires. Most men never gaze into the catacombs and never glimpse the dark side of the moon.

Sinclair was not like other men; he not only glimpsed the dark side, he held a microscope to it; he not only gazed into the catacombs, he lived there - with the rats and ghosts and skulls stacked from floor to ceiling, tomb after endless tomb.

There were times in Sinclair's life that he could have done almost anything from bankrupting a nation to the assassination of a president. He could have killed or been killed and he no longer cared.

Roman Mason was not the only one to drop down a hole after the election. Sinclair dropped out and came to terms with his only surviving nemesis: death. He realized that everything he ever did was wrong. The sum total of his life on earth was a persistent burden on human kind, a force not unlike a tidal wave or tsunami, a clear and present danger to every living thing.

He was a carrier of the seed of death, a plague that contaminated everything he touched. Knowing that he was dying, a victim of his own disease, and that he could never hope to undo the damage, he swore that if he had a chance he would do whatever he could.

In his dying days, Sinclair was determined to strike a balance. If he could somehow accomplish a great good, he could avenge his former life and leave this wretched earth no better and no worse for his existence.

He had moved beyond the normal constraints of moral upbringing, social values or the tenets of religion. He had moved beyond guilt and pleasure to the cold, calculated equation of cause and effect. All that mattered now was how the world changed.

From the moment he heard the news that Mason was back in the field of play, the air grew cleaner, the colors of life more vibrant, and the music sweeter. Rome was a man of ambition, a dreamer, a seeker of dreams, and a man who did not settle for less than all he could achieve.

The essential difference between Mason and Sinclair was that Mason was constrained by virtue. His strength was his weakness. He could be counted on to do the right thing – save the girl, rescue the child or climb the tree to pull down the crying cat. If not for that most singular flaw, reflected Sinclair, Mason could have ruled the world.

Their last project ended in failure but even failure was sweet when it reached for the heavens. If Rome was back, hope was alive. The universe of possibilities was expanding and no man or woman, however powerful or protected, was secure. At the very least, there was a promise of drama that would breathe momentary life into his dying limbs.

Sinclair leaned back in his easy chair, took a drag on his Cuban cigar, sipped his exquisite French red wine and allowed the music of Tchaikovsky to wash over him. The chessboard was set, the opening moves planned and plotted, and the players in their respective places. He watched the smoke circle, hover and settle like a cloud of foreboding. He saw the shadow of death and allowed a contented smile to invade his sullen mood.

"You will have your revenge," he said.

"Come what may, time and the hour run through the roughest day."

He felt the darkness surrounding him. Outside his palatial estate overlooking greater Seattle, a storm was brewing, the darkness within joining the darkness without, and the dark knight, comforted in his darkened, fire lit room, yielded to the sweet temptation of sleep. He succumbed and let himself fall into the web of dreams.

He closed his eyes and saw a light. Fighting an impulse that had ruled his conduct through decades of political machinations, in fighting, vendetta campaigns, character assassinations, smears and deceptions, he moved forward toward the light and what he saw buried him in shame:

He saw himself dying...alone.

THE CORE

Fatal Flaw
The Rust Principle
The Ground Up
A Lucky Man

Summers in Seattle were always comfortably mild. The cool winds of the northern Pacific swept through the Strait of Juan de Fuca, channeling through the Sound, protecting the burgeoning metropolis that ran from Tacoma to Vancouver.

Something changed. The summer of 2005 was oppressively hot, sweltering hot, mind numbing and punishing hot. It was as if the entire northwest was somehow transported to the southeast, where the August air was molasses thick. Whether it was a freak event or a foreshadowing of global climate change, the people were lethargic, edgy and ready to explode.

Margaret Thomas did not know what to think when Rome Mason requested an appointment. History was rich between Rome and Maggie. Rome pushed her to run for congress and helped manage a successful campaign. After the election, they drifted apart. Rome had no taste for the Washington crowd and Maggie was determined to prove that an independent congresswoman could deliver. Maggie was re-elected in 2004 and Rome dropped off the edge the world.

That was Rome. His highs were the stars and his lows were rock bottom. Their relationship fed Maggie's passion and strengthened her resolve. A well compensated corporate attorney, she needed someone or something to reawaken the dreams of youth. She was in danger of losing herself in the money machine of a successful career. Along came Roman Mason with a dream of reshaping the political landscape and a plan for making it happen.

She knew there would come a time when he stepped back into her life. Beyond that, she did not know what to expect. Life did not stand still. There were other men in her life. With Rome, it was best to keep expectations in the rearview mirror.

Speaking to him over the phone, she sensed that the fire was burning white hot. The dream was the same but the plan was more realistic. He was putting together a core group of advisors with the immediate goal of organizing a unity conference of independent political and activist organizations.

To achieve their objectives, they would have to break the anarchist mold, find common ground and secure financial backing. With an antiwar, anti-oil and anti-corporate globalization agenda, they would have to secure that backing from like-minded individuals who had profited from the same capitalistic system they would now oppose.

They needed a core group capable of defining common ground, mapping a long-term strategy and seeking out non-traditional sources of wealth. They needed Maggie not only for her political mind and legal expertise but as a model of the kind of success they were seeking: an independent who refused corporate funding. If all went as planned, Maggie would serve as the face and spokesperson for the cause.

The first meeting was in the back room of a Seattle jazz joint called The Monastery in honor of the legendary jazzman Thelonious Monk. Its thick stone walls and high wooden ceilings with large exposed rafters gave it the feeling of an old European castle. It was early evening and the sound of a jazz trio and their appreciative audience slipped through the cracks of a majestic wooden door. When he was not on sabbatical, it was Roman Mason's favorite haunt. On the rarest occasions, which no one seemed to witness first hand, he was said to join in a jam with his battered tenor sax.

On the drive to The Monastery, Maggie remembered listening to him play that old horn, often for hours without relief, on the balcony overlooking the city, at his Olympic estate over the rocky cliffs of the northern Pacific or on the porch of his cabin on the Sound. It was the sound of mourning. It was the dirge of a New Orleans jazz funeral. It was diving off the edge and discovering the inner depths of his subconscious mind. It was dying and being born.

Maggie felt a twinge of remorse and let it go. It was a reminder that life with Rome was both sweet and sorrowful. It was profound and disturbing. Rome had come to terms with his life. He believed it was a means of tapping another world, a key to his creativity, but he had seen and suffered the toll it took on those around him. He would no longer inflict his disease on those he loved. Maggie was the last.

When Maggie walked in and moved through the hall to the back room, with the sound of jazz and the smile of familiar faces, her knees went soft. She let her heart remember the softness, the passion, the glory and the love.

She walked in where the others were already seated at the round table. She felt the pull, the attraction, the weight of desire and she could tell by the light in Rome's eyes, even more than the smile on his face, he felt it too. Old loves never die – not the ones that dance to the rhythm of truth.

Maggie was seated and Rome introduced the group of five that would for now form the core of an organization. Each was at least aware of the others' work. There was Roy Jones, a passionate writer for the cause with an astute political mind. There was Amy Goodall, a dynamic activist and organizer. There was John Sinclair, an operative of the highest order. There was Rome, the man who made things happen, and there was Maggie, one of only two independent members of congress.

There was room for up to four more members of the core but that would have to wait for events to unfold. For now, Rome thought it best that they possessed a familiarity that eliminated the need for explorations. They shared the same objective: to break the back of the two-party hammerlock on American politics. They were all weary of symbolic campaigns and they all understood the nature of the game.

Rome laid out a plan like the first draft of a long story. They would build an organization from the ground up. They would raise funds from a broad base of support and target winnable elections at the state and local levels. They would build a financial base of support the old fashioned way: by winning. They would recruit and train a new generation of activists, dissidents and politically savvy operatives. They would think long term and guard against the divisions that traditionally sabotaged populist and democratic movements.

Rome would be the behind the scene center point, coordinating the varied branches. Roy would be the message maker, the propagandist, the communicator. Amy would form a bridge to the activist world, channeling protest into grassroots political campaigns. Sinclair would head the electoral branch, targeting elections, recruiting candidates and running campaigns. Maggie would be their public voice, their connection in Washington and advisor to the independent movement's most promising candidates.

Amy: *What about the war? What about free trade, immigration, labor exploitation, global warming, civil rights and civil liberties…?*

Rome: *Those are issues with clear solutions and ones we can all agree on.*

Amy: *What takes precedence? The issues or the political agenda?*

Rome: *We gave everything to the antiwar movement. What do we have to show? The organization and the core cause crumbled yet the war goes on. The one thing we must all agree on is that we can never allow that to happen again. We're building an institution to challenge the power structure. We're building a movement that doesn't end when the warlords move on to their next target. We're building a cause that can be handed to the next generation. Nothing is more important.*

Roy: *Many activists have hit bottom. They want to move beyond protest to active resistance.*

Sinclair with a knowing grin: *We support them. Resistance is powerful; aggression is counterproductive.*

Rome: *We don't want a revolution. We want evolution.*

Maggie: *There will be another terrorist attack. That is the central event on the political horizon and the trillion-dollar question is: How do we respond? What do we do then?*

Rome: *With empathy but without compromise.*

Amy: *We accuse the power duopoly of allowing it to happen for their own political and economic gain.*

Sinclair: *We can't know when it will happen. Only that it will happen and when it does, there will be a backlash, another wave of oppression. We must be prepared for all contingencies and every step must be taken with that inevitability in mind.*

A solemn silence conveyed a general agreement, suggesting that everything that needed saying had been. A superb Italian wine was poured and Roy proposed a toast.

Evolution, not revolution! It's about time.

They drank, talked, laughed and cried into the early hours of the morn, sharing their dreams, their nightmares, their hopes and fantasies, until only Rome and Maggie remained. They drank from the same chalice, dreamed the same dreams, shared the same fears and felt the same pull that tied them together in another life.

Maggie had a week before she needed to return to the nation's capital. Rome had no obligations save those he imposed on himself. They were free, as free as they had ever been, and if they chose to live in the moment, it was nobody's business but their own.

They took a cab to the wharf, a ferry across the Sound, where a driver waited to take them to Rome's estate on the western side of the peninsula. Here, overlooking a rocky cliff, where the waves betrayed the pounding heartbeat of the earth, where Rome discovered his cause and where his love for Maggie and hers for Rome blossomed and flourished with a bond that would outlast their mortal lives.

They held each other in the arms of undying affection, allowed the past to recede, and rediscovered the meaning of life on earth. When Rome and Maggie came together, no one else mattered. The cause remained – it was always there—but Rome only had eyes for Maggie and Maggie for Rome.

Holding her in his arms, in the sweet honey afterglow of love, the taste fresh on his lips, the scent hovering in the air, he had only one thought: Oh, what a lucky man he was.

KATRINA

August 29, 2005
A Terrorist Attack
Prayers for New Orleans

Nearly four years after the attack on the World Trade Center, the Pentagon and an unknown third target, there was a second terrorist attack and the conspiracy to cover up the truth was no less determined.

Katrina was a category three hurricane that missed New Orleans yet the devastation was complete. The lowlands of the Ninth Ward, Gentilly and St. Bernard Parrish were buried under a wall of water, hundreds died, hundreds more would never be counted, and tens of thousands were scattered across the land like third world refugees.

It was not the storm that buried New Orleans. It was not the hand of god or the wheel of fortune that sealed her fate. It was negligence, intentional human negligence at the highest levels of government.

What is the definition of a terrorist attack? If a man or an agency knows what will happen when an inevitable convergence of events occurs and not only fails to act but acts in a manner that will maximize the disaster, is it really any different than flying a passenger plane into a tower of civilians?

The Army Corps of Engineers knew what they were doing when they used inadequate funds to contract inadequate work to rebuild and reinforce the levees that stood between the poor black folk of New Orleans and a watery grave. Renowned for their genius around the world, the Corps ingeniously erected a façade that created an illusion of strength. The Corps knew it would topple when tested and the Corps knew it would be tested.

When a lonely meteorologist warned that Katrina could spell catastrophe the Corps did not sound the alarm. When there was still a chance at mass evacuation, the Corps stood down. The Corps had a job to do but that job was not to protect the poor of New Orleans; it was to guard their reputation as they skimmed funds from the levees, bridges and dams of America so they could build fortresses for international oil companies in Iraq.

The Army Corps of Engineers was hoping that Katrina would hit dead on at full force so that no one would notice or care that the levees were defective. They were counting on the president to attribute the massive destruction to an act of god and the hammer of inevitable fate. They were counting on every expression of empathy to be followed by a qualifier: There was nothing we could do.

They were not counting on day after day of suffering people pleading for help while the government's representatives threw up their hands in ignorance. They were not counting on floating corpses and an endless parade of homeless people wading through toxic waters to the convention center or the

Superdome where no help was waiting.

Before Katrina, not even the most venomous critic could have imagined an American leader so heartless, so indifferent, so out of touch with the common man that he failed to notice his people were dying.

We watched the events unfold, the slowness of federal response, the absence of the guard, the insensitivity of our president, the absolute lack of urgency in the face of disaster, and we knew it was a crime against human dignity that would endure the ages. The entire nation and much of the world witnessed in stark, vivid detail what it was to live poor and black in America.

We had a government that could run the river backwards rather than allow an unfortunate brain dead woman the dignity of a private and natural death but could not raise a hand to deliver food, water and medical supplies to the birthplace of jazz.

Katrina was a terrorist attack that ripped at the cover of class warfare. Like the targets of our bombs in foreign nations, the poor were mostly dark skinned and faceless. They were not a part of the American dream; they were a part of the American cesspool – or so they seemed to our privileged overlords.

The Corps of Engineers was right that New Orleans would be tested; New Orleans would be tested in Houston, Nashville, Austin, Chicago, Los Angeles, New York and Salt Lake City. The city of jazz would be tested from Portland, Oregon to Portland, Maine, from the Golden Gate to the shining beacon on a hill. New Orleans would be tested in every two-cent town with a television and a diner.

Every militant Islamist was pointing to CNN and saying: See how they treat their own – and they have oil too. Yes, New Orleans is rich in oil. It possesses an abundant supply just off its marshy coast. It has so much oil that if it were a foreign nation and its Diaspora were refugees as the media proclaimed, New Orleans would be richer than the United Arab Emirates and it would have no need of our assistance.

New Orleans is rich in culture and irony – jazz and the blues. How ironic that its people were shipped to the four corners of the nation as immigrant Hispanics at substandard wages were hired for the clean up. The powers knew the citizens of New Orleans would insist on rebuilding their schools, hospitals and homes while the illegal immigrants would simply do as they were told. New Orleans would become a Disneyland, a new Mecca for corporate greed, a haven for casinos and high-rise hotels. There would be no room for the poor black folk who were the heart of the city of jazz.

New Orleans would never be the same but the powers were fools if they thought it would go down without a fight. They had unleashed an enduring heartache that would translate into words and music, a story that would be told for a thousand years.

Once there was a city whose citizens were a ragtag collection of slaves and semi-slaves, the misfits and miscreants of a nation whose ambition was larger than its conscience. Once there was a city where blacks, whites, and every shade of gray learned to live together in the harmony of jazz. Once there was a city where French and English were mixed in a steamy brew of Cajun and Creole and the dialects of the Louisiana bayou. Once there was a city that gave birth to the finest music and the most diverse culture the world has ever known. Once there was a city where the poor were not poor for they possessed that richness of spirit and culture and music and tolerance that was the envy of all others.

Once there was a city of jazz. No more.

Mourn for the people who lost their lives. Mourn for the people who lost their souls. Mourn for the people who lost their homes. Mourn for the people who will never return. Mourn for the people who will never stop mourning. Mourn for the people who never knew New Orleans before the storm.

Katrina was a terrorist attack, a conspiracy of indifference, the "shock and awe" campaign of a war on the poor.

Mourn for New Orleans, the most genuine and culturally rich city in the world, and take a solemn vow never to forget.

One year from Katrina do not forget that the Ninth Ward is still barren.

Two years from Katrina do not forget that New Orleans was once more than Mardi Gras and the French Quarters.

Three years from Katrina do not forget that the people of New Orleans are still poor but they no longer have the comfort of home.

Ten years from Katrina do not forget that New Orleans was buried in water by an act of man, not of god.

Twenty years from Katrina, remember that New Orleans was once a raw, thriving city where art and artists were born.

Thirty years from Katrina remember New Orleans and mourn.

A CALL TO ARMS

Global Activism
Requiem New Orleans

Katrina was a call to arms. Every activist in the western world witnessed a pause, a freeze, a silencing of time, and stood in rapt attention. Here was a nation at war, inflicting crimes and atrocities on innocent peoples abroad, yet it stood down when its own people were suffering.

September 11 finally had an answer and her name was Katrina.

Sara Kent was in Paris when Katrina buried New Orleans. She had just visited a memorial to the communard, a turn of the century failed attempt to liberate France. There, where nine citizens of the republic were lined up and gunned down, lilies grew and the story of human sacrifice was told.

Sara was a citizen of the world. After the 2000 election, she cashed in her earnings as an attorney at law and became an artist. She tended to the Bohemian in writing, drawing, painting, sculpting, and so was drawn to Paris and Prague. Everywhere she went she found cafes, pubs and taverns where political discourse thrived.

She remained active. It was in her blood. It was in

her art. She was in Vienna when September 11 came down. Like all of her brethren, she gasped at the horror of destruction and death and again at the horror that would follow. She was in Amsterdam when the invasion of Afghanistan was launched. She was in Prague when the neocon warlords of the Bush White House built their case for war with Iraq. She uncovered documents that helped reveal the lie of a secret meeting between Iraqi agents and Al Qaeda extremists. She was in London for the largest antiwar gathering in recorded history.

Sara was profoundly disturbed by how little their efforts made an impact on the governments that were supposed to represent them. Like Rome, she turned away from overt politics in despair. Unlike Rome, she did not seek refuge or atonement in isolation; she sought redemption in art.

Sara's art was always political. She did not guide her work in that direction; it simply emerged. She reflected the duplicity of feckless leaders, the shameless greed behind lofty ideals, the nameless dead and massive destruction in the name of freedom, justice and democracy.

For three days, she did nothing but watch the citizens of New Orleans suffer and survive as they exposed the lie of government compassion. For three nights, she did nothing but listen to jazz and commiserate with fellow Parisians, native and expatriate, who felt a deep and enduring kinship with the city that defined America's soul. For three days, she cursed CNN and extolled public officials to do something, anything, to deliver water, food and medical supplies. For three days, she felt a rising anger and shame at being an American.

A PATRIOT DIRGE

On the fourth day, she contacted Amy Goodall, an activist she met in London, to ask what she could do. Amy painted a grim picture, explaining what was happening in the states. They had sent many teams to New Orleans, builders, carpenters, electricians, organizers, doctors, nurses, skilled volunteers but all were turned back at the gates. The media was dead wrong on one key fact: Security forces were there but they were not charged with helping or protecting the people, they were there to keep help out.

Something was going on in New Orleans that was rotten to the core. If Sara wanted to help, the best thing she could do would be to head an investigation and legal team. She was afraid that the poor people being evacuated to centers all over the country would never be allowed to return. She was afraid that the insurance companies would steal people's homes and property. She was afraid that the land cleared by Katrina and the defective levees was already reserved for other purposes. The poor were being evicted without just compensation.

As they shared their thoughts and tears over the suffering people of New Orleans, the subject turned to common acquaintances, most notably Roman Mason.

"He's back," said Amy, "and he's on fire."

"Maybe the best thing you can do is call Rome and come home."

They talked about old times and better days. They talked about the changes in their lives, Amy's marriage and Sara's art. They talked about politics and they talked about New Orleans. Conspiracy theories were thriving. Anything was preferable than believing the apparent cold-hearted truth: that the government did not care.

Bush was a second term president accountable to no one. That he and his people did not care about blacks was obvious, that they did not care about the poor was clear to anyone who looked beyond the rough façade of a little rich boy who never worked an honest day's labor in his life. New Orleans brought it all home.

Even now, on the fourth day of suffering and neglect, their token appearances in the ravaged region, the president's pledge in Jackson Square, with the statue of Indian killer Andrew Jackson, the man who singularly enforced genocide on the Cherokee nation, rang shallow and false.

Did it matter? Historical ironies were lost on a people that did not know history.

They talked until there was nothing more to say, then they cried a river of tears, wished each other well and said goodbye.

Sara went into a deep depression. All the emotions she held back or channeled into her art came spilling forth. She had taken a vow to leave politics behind her. She was an artist now. She was committed to the cause from a different perspective, one that did not require collaboration with others.

She knew the moment she put down the phone, her life was evolving once again. She knew that she would return to the states and the low down universe of political and legal manipulations. She knew she could not remain above the fray. It was a call to arms and she could not refrain.

Expatriates around the world and activists at home were hearing the same call and answering in their own ways. Sara's was after all not that different from Rome's way. She would dive into the liquid depths of darkness, morbid, terrifying darkness. She would hit rock bottom and descend further, darker and lower than she had ever dove before. She would shed her skin like the fabled serpent and she would emerge stronger, larger and ready for battle.

She knew the way forward but she did not fear for the people of New Orleans, the lower ninth ward, Gentilly and St. Bernard Parrish, would comfort her. They would suffer together and together they would survive. Together, they would build the strength and unity of survival. Together they would construct a bridge to the land of hope and promise.

If they did not succeed, they would die knowing they did everything in their power, everything in their collective imagination, everything that could be done to find the light of justice and build a better world.

THE STRANGE CASE OF SIMON JUNEAU

The Limits of Conscience
Redemption in a Box

Hands trembling, tears welling in eyes of remorse, a veteran of four decades of political warfare, a little man with thin, snow white hair and wire rim glasses to compensate his fading vision, Simon Juneau crouched over a computer, pecking the keyboard one key at a time.

In the barren desert of Southeast Arizona, Juneau was as far removed from the political world as imagination would allow. Like many of his colleagues, he was coaxed from retirement once in 2000 and once again in 2004.

He had hoped for nothing more than to spend his remaining days on earth seeking solace with the silent desert. Instead, he was summoned by the irresistible call of history. In Florida, he worked his magic behind the scenes, orchestrating protests, manipulating media coverage, leaking memos and inventing poll data.

It was Juneau who convinced the overmatched Democrats that they should limit their demands to a few key counties, thus sacrificing the moral high ground and departing from the dictates of Floridian law. A statewide recount would have handed the election and the White House to Al Gore but a limited recount in counties largely controlled by Democrats would leave the Bush victory in place.

Juneau often wondered how stupid the Democrats could be. They were lawyered up but their operatives went missing. He wondered if in fact they were in on the fix.

What happened in Florida? It was a conspiracy to defraud the American electorate. It was a disgrace to American democracy. The Republicans played hardball, promising a scorched earth unless the case was allowed to be played out in the courts on their own terms. The Democrats, with a thousand black tie attorneys, naively thought they could win on the issue of hanging chads.

When the case was thrown up to the most partisan Supreme Court in history, the fix was in. What should have been an indictment of Governor Jeb Bush and his lackey Secretary of State, a case of fraud and disenfranchisement on a scale unseen since the days of Jim Crow, was never heard.

A corrupt corporate media never told the real story.

Simon Juneau watched the events of September 11, 2001, and all that followed with the skepticism of an old man who had seen too much. He watched the bombardment of Afghanistan and the invasion of Iraq and he cursed the day he was born.

If he had not worked his magic in Florida, perhaps the Democrats would have prevailed. Assuming a terrorist attack was somehow preordained, how would President Albert Gore have responded? Whatever else, he was certain we would not have gone to war with a country that had nothing to do with the attack on this nation.

Juneau was a tortured soul but there was little he could do until the 2004 election, when the call went out to all operatives to come to Ohio for what seemed a reprise of Florida 2000. It was his chance at redemption and what he learned in a matter of days was more than enough to turn the republic on its head.

No one was more disappointed than Simon Juneau when Democrat John Kerry yielded the election without a fight. He felt cheated. At the end of a long and distinguished career, he felt the sting of a betrayal so profound it overshadowed all else. He no longer perceived himself as an instrument of democracy; he was a conspirator to treason.

There was no other word. Stealing an election was treason to its core. Handing the reins of the most powerful government on earth to a group of maniacs and an ambitious boy king was a crime against civilization for which hundreds of thousands if not millions would pay with their lives.

Beads of cold sweat ran down his wrinkled forehead as he tapped the last few keystrokes. He copied the file to disk, took a breath, removed it and sealed it with a cassette recording in a padded envelope. He made another copy, scribbled a note, sealed it in a separate envelope, and then sat back and tried to restore calm.

Here was a man who had gripped the hands of monumental American leaders – Nixon, Ford, Johnson, Reagan, Bush – yet now, at the twilight of his journey through life, he could not stop his hands from shaking.

Eyes drooping, body aching, he wanted nothing more than to lie down for a long rest but he was afraid that if he yielded even for a moment he would lose the will to act. The curse of his advancing years, years of loneliness and yearning since his life's partner passed seven years prior, was that the pangs of conscience gave in too easily to rationalizations of indifference. If the world was determined to drive off the edge to unending nightmares, who was he to stand in the way?

He gathered the envelopes in his still trembling hands and made the drive to the nearest post office in Bisbee.

What happened in Ohio was very similar to what happened in Florida four years earlier but with a twist. In the days and weeks preceding the election, the numbers made it clear it would come down to Ohio. With the Secretary of State firmly in the Republican pocket, all the measures of disenfranchisement were in place: last-minute changes in polling locations, inadequate personnel and voting machines in black and Democratic districts, threats and challenges at the polling places, eviction of election monitors and the purging of black voters from the voting lists.

When it seemed, in the final hours, that all their efforts would be in vain, the call went out for Operation Chameleon to be executed and, along with it, the last remnants of American democracy would die.

On Election Day, Americans would see report after report of voter fraud in Ohio even after the exit polls announced a comfortable victory for John Kerry. Hundreds of voters would report witnessing the on-screen conversion of votes for Kerry into votes for George W. Bush. Thousands of disgruntled, protesting voters were told to fill out conditional ballots that would never be counted.

Despite a mountain of evidence, John Kerry conceded the election on November 6. To his supporters, it appeared that the operatives had convinced their candidate that he would go down in history as the man who saved American democracy by refusing to allow a repeat of the 2000 debacle.

The truth was infinitely more insidious. John Kerry and the younger Bush (like his father) were members of the same elite club of international overlords. They had carefully constructed the Kerry campaign so that he could carry on with the war in Iraq for four more years but in the final hours they decided they needed more. They required four more years of the neocon philosophy of perpetual war to seal their claim for permanent control of Middle Eastern oil. They wanted more than a Democrat could reasonably deliver.

In the final analysis, John Kerry was in on the fix and Simon Juneau held the smoking gun – compelling and incontrovertible evidence of deliberate and bipartisan election fraud: recorded conversations with Ohio Secretary of State Kenneth Blackwell, Walden O'Dell of Diebold Election Systems, Karl Rove, Dick Cheney, George Bush and Kerry, himself.

If not for the trust they placed in him as a tried and true operative, if not for the part he played in Florida 2000, he would not have been in a position to document the greatest election fraud since the days of Tammany Hall or Richard Daley and the Chicago machine. He would have settled for watching Arizona sunsets over evening cocktails with coyotes and creatures of the desert as his only companions.

The Grand Old Party assumed Simon Juneau was one of them, a man so corrupted he was immune to moral constraint. It did not occur to them that even he had a line he would not cross and that line was drawn across the state of Ohio. He was astonished at the silence of the media and sickened that the political process was so poisoned that all the king's men and women could witness the overt stealing of a presidential election and stand down.

He understood there was no distinction between parties and little distinction between the political establishment and Mafia crime families. Even those who played a part in the Kennedy assassinations recognized a line of restraint. Politics were always dirty on both sides of the aisle but there remained a line one did not cross. Now it seemed that line had ceased to exist.

So an elderly politico, guilty on so many levels of corruption and fraud, decided to take action. Despite everything he had done and everything he had witnessed and condoned by silent affirmation, he still considered himself a decent man. He believed in a divine presence. He believed that he was put on earth to do a job and to fulfill his destiny. He now believed his destiny was to blow the lid off a truth that sickened him to the core.

He felt like the Jews of Nazi Germany who survived the holocaust by "passing" as gentiles, even to the point of becoming card carrying members of the Nazi Party. If he could have stopped Hitler, he was certain he would have. If he could have stopped the assassination of a president, he would not have failed to act. He could do nothing to alter history but at this late stage of life, he was given a last chance at redemption and he took it.

What Simon Juneau did not know, as he deposited his envelopes in the mail drop of the Bisbee post office, was that his file, sans sweat and tears, was already in the hands of his adversaries and former colleagues. As much as he had adapted to the technological age, he did not realize how easily computer files were tapped, even when they were never sent over the web.

Later that evening, about one in the morning, when an old friend showed up with a couple of his lackeys, Simon knew exactly what was happening. The time for negotiation was closed. Sam Tilden was a man in a box. He was not empowered to make choices. Like an SS officer, he did what he was told. The only discretion his superiors allowed him was methodology.

Like Juneau, Tilden was an old timer, a veteran of political warfare, and he was familiar with Juneau's work and reputation. Out of respect, he allowed the old master a few more hours of life. The lackeys waited outside while the old warriors settled by the fire to talk old times and lament that it all came down to this.

The hushed sounds of night, a warm breeze, the scent of sage and the cold blue light of a desert moon slipped though open balcony doors with a majestic view of the desert night.

"Where there is no honor," reflected the killer, "there can be no satisfaction."

"Yes," replied Juneau. "And all the satisfaction we once felt in a job well executed has withered like an old man's desire."

"Speak for yourself," said Tilden.

Tilden was no fool. He knew better than to become infected by the disease that killed Simon Juneau. He made a choice long ago to let go of his conscience. The best he could do was to deliver fate with some small measure of grace.

He produced a small leather pouch from his breast pocket, pulled out a capsule and poured the contents into Juneau's finest red wine. Within minutes, Juneau's mind was drifting through a maze of memories until it settled on one last thought: his last act, his assertion of conscience and his redemption now rested in the words printed on two envelopes in the Bisbee post office: The Editor of the New York Times and John Sinclair, Esquire.

He smiled at the thought and let his spirit float away.

Simon Juneau was dead.

BURN BABY BURN

A Convergence of Circumstance
The Making of a Terrorist

If there is such a thing as fate, it is the product of a convergence of circumstance. A leader or a philanthropist is not born or educated to that end and a man does not become a terrorist overnight.

Miguel Estrada was a promising youth. Inquisitive, curious, energetic, loyal to his friends and devoted to his family, his childhood was marked by tragedy when his parents were caught in an immigration sting and deported to Mexico. His aunt Mirabel, who had lost her husband to an industrial accident, raised him as if he was her own. She had two sons and a daughter but did not hesitate to take Miguel into her home, feed him, clothe him, and teach him the values she personified.

From the ages of six to nine, he knew his parents, his little brother Juan and his older sister Esmeralda only by the weekly letters his mother wrote. She often included photographs that chronicled the passing of time. Juanito the toddler became Juan the schoolboy while Esmeralda grew from a schoolgirl to a budding young woman.

Miguel collected his mother's letters and stored them in a wooden box. He would spend hours reading them and gazing at the pictures, counting the days when he would be reunited with the family. His mother always promised the day would come and hoped it would come soon. His aunt was willing to deliver him back to Guadalajara but his mother was determined that at least one of her children would grow up to become an American citizen. It was her dream that her children could find a better life in the north and that one day the United States of America would welcome them all.

Shortly after his ninth birthday, the letters stopped coming. Aunt Mirabel explained that hard times had come to Jalisco and it was impossible for his mother to keep writing. It would be several years before she told him the truth.

The family had paid a coyote to provide papers and take them across the border through the Arizona desert. It was impossible to trace their route but they were never seen or heard from again. Some said a devious coyote, an unscrupulous deviant interested only in money, dumped them in the desert without water or food. Others said the border patrol or vigilantes taking "justice" into their own hands had done the deed.

In the end, it did not matter. He no longer had a family. All that remained were memories, a box of letters and fading photographs.

Miguel became embittered and angry. For the first time, he began to have trouble at school and he brought that trouble home. He fought with the other children and when Aunt Mirabel disciplined him, he complained that she treated him differently than her natural children.

It broke Mirabel's heart but she understood his

anguish. From the loss she had suffered in her own life, she knew that only time could heal wounds of the soul.

Miguel held on to his anger. His anger was his connection to the family he lost. His anger was his love and as long as he held on to it, they would live within him. He swore an oath to his god, his life and all that he cherished that he would not lose them again.

He wore his anger like a brand on his forehead, always visible, always glaring through his dark soulful eyes. It attracted others to him who felt as he did. There was Victor with his *norteno* markings, Corazon with his scars, and the angry girls Annabel and Dulce who understood what boys wanted before they should have.

By the time he became a teenager, he and his friends had found the real outlaws, the ones that dealt in drugs, workers, tobacco, alcohol – anything that could be sold or transported at a profit. They served as lookouts and messengers but more than that they were being watched and groomed for the roles they would soon play.

Ironically, it was the old man who ran the house where Miguel and his buddies hung out who turned him around. El Viejo Marcos was the rare individual who survived in a game that did not allow survivors. Unlike most of his fallen compadres, Marcos knew when to turn away and how to back down without losing face. He understood that respect, more than guns and money, was the one commodity that was indispensable.

In the summer of his sixteenth birthday, Miguel was not surprised that the old man called him over to his shaded porch for a conversation over ice tea. The house was on the outskirts of Denver where an old man could sit on his porch, gazing out at the expanse of land, and wonder why there was not enough for everyone.

Marcos and Miguel had many conversations on this porch about everything under the sun. They talked about poverty and immigration and industrial waste and war and the role of government in easing the sorrows of its citizens. They talked about the failings of human beings in caring for the planet and why the corporate elites no longer took an interest.

The people are sleeping, the old man explained. *They give us drugs and guns and playthings and mesmerize us with their magic so that the people no longer believe it has anything to do with us.*

He would speak aloud the words that fell from his mind, then grow silent and study to see if Miguel understood. He did. The old man understood about anger as well and never advised the boy to give it up or grow beyond it. He told him to hang on to it and to embrace it whenever the gringos tried to put him in his place.

The first thing the old man noticed about Miguel was that he always carried a book in the back pocket of his oversized jeans. He never asked about it until today.

Miguel grimaced and said it was nothing but the old man insisted so he pulled it out and placed on the table. Marcos gazed at it and held it to his nose as if he could inhale its contents. *This is a good book,* he said. *Many hands held it before it found its way to yours. Read it to me.*

The muscles in his face tightened and he glanced around as if to see if anyone was watching. It was a book of poetry by Pablo Neruda, love poems, not the kind of literature that outlaws would read if they read at all. If it was anyone else, he would have refused and walked away. Anyone else and he would have known it was a joke, meant to put him in his place, but the old man was like a grandfather to him. If he could not trust Marcos, he could never trust anyone.

Hands trembling, he opened the book, cleared his throat and began to read.

Cuerpo de mujer, blancas Colinas, muslos blancos,
Te pareces al mundo en tu actitud de entrega…

He paused to study the old man, as the old man had so often regarded him, eyes closed, head rolled back, listening with his heart. He read on deep into the night, when the old man allowed him to stop with the promise that he would return the next day to finish the reading. He did so and as he finished the last page, closing the book and placing it on the table, he discovered the old man was crying silent tears, tears of memory, regret, sorrow and pain.

You have a gift, he said, not bothering to wipe the tears from his face. *You have the gift of understanding what you cannot understand.* He held the book in his great hands and pressed it to his face. *Now my understanding joins with yours,* he said to Neruda through the mirror of his book.

I have spoken to your Aunt Mirabel. Again, the muscles of his body tightened. His aunt knew who Marcos was. Miguel would be greeted at home with a lecture on the company he kept. *I asked her if you were a good student. She replied that you were when you chose to be.*

Perhaps, I replied, he needs incentive.

Miguel relaxed, letting the tension flow from the

center of his being through his body and out his limbs. In this world of hard cold realities, where parents were deported and died in the desert, it was the last thing he expected: human kindness.

Marcos was illiterate and he had chosen Miguel to receive the opportunity he most cherished but was denied. He offered a college education on the condition that Miguel earn it. He did. He completed high school with sterling grades and attended the University of Colorado on a full scholarship from the outlaws, earning degrees in literature and political science.

The anger never left him but he used it as the old man advised. He channeled it into his studies. It was the anger that would lead almost inevitably to trouble. He joined several political activist student organizations. Some of them were considered radical even in the ultra left environment of Boulder, Colorado.

One group that railed against foreign policy, global trade policy and environmental destruction, decided to go beyond the normal methods of protest. They were determined to burn down the summer home of the CEO of Halliburton, a company that specialized in the spoils of war.

They were caught before they could do any harm. The other students, sons and daughters of the elite, were given a hand slap, six months probation and released but Miguel was held on handful of felony charges. In addition, there were questions regarding his immigration status and the validity of the documents he used to enroll at the university.

With a promise to make things uncomfortable for several high ranking officers in the Denver Police Department, El Viejo Marcos negotiated Miguel's release on the condition that he enlist in the military.

If he signs on the dotted line we'll wipe the slate clean.

Miguel took the deal, volunteering for service in the United States Army. At the time, it did not seem unreasonable. Not only would it cleanse his record, he was assured it would clear his citizenship status.

It was August 2001. In a month, he would be preparing for war in Afghanistan. In less than two years, he would be deployed to Iraq.

A DECLARATION OF INDEPENDENTS

A New Politics
A Party of Pragmatism
Drafting a Political Philosophy

We are pragmatic populist progressive libertarians. We are pragmatic in our approach to political change, populist in that we pledge to listen to the people even when it disturbs or enrages us, progressive in that we represent the working people and libertarian in social policies because we believe that no government should impose on the private affairs of its citizens.

The pragmatism of politics dictates that we will not push for programs, reforms or legislation that has no realistic chance of being enacted. For example, we recognize that government sponsored health insurance (what some call a single-payer system) is the ultimate solution to our health and medical care crisis but we also know that there is not a sufficient base of support at present to overcome the inevitable rightwing charge of "socialized medicine" – no matter how specious the accusation.

The politics of pragmatism means that in districts heavily influenced by religious institutions it is sacrificial to advocate same sex marriage or a woman's right to abortion. In such cases we advocate neutrality, even pledge to abstain, in deference to other social, political and economic interests.

The politics of pragmatism does not require pandering. We will not abstain from stating our positions, expressing our values or explaining our beliefs. We will answer all questions openly and honestly without regard for political expediency.

We will listen to the people. We will listen as mainstream politicians listen to lobbyists and special interests – as if our political lives depended on it. We will address all issues of greatest concern to the people. We will find solutions that we believe have the greatest potential to alleviate today's problems without creating new problems in the future. We will balance the common good against the rights of individuals.

On the issue of national security, we propose a reasoned approach. We will not sacrifice individual civil liberties. We will not ignore the direct relationship between American foreign policy and terrorism. We will advocate a foreign policy that respects the rights and cultural differences of other nations. We will end the policy of American exceptionalism that claims the right to attack other nations without provocation, that exempts America from the universal laws of all nations and that demands of others what we would not submit to ourselves. We will support diplomacy, international law and international institutions that provide an alternative to military intervention for the resolution of conflicts.

As we strengthen international institutions and lengthen their reach, we will shut down unnecessary military bases and channel those resources to enhance our chances of survival on the planet.

On the issue of immigration, we recognize the

concerns that an open border brings but we do not agree that a wall separating us from our neighbors is a reasonable solution. We cannot ignore the fundamental truth that nearly all of us are the offspring of unwanted invaders. A wall is the multi-billion dollar non-solution of pandering politicians who do not want to see the problem go away. If there were no immigration problem, how would they defend the policies they have promoted for two decades? If they could not blame illegal immigrants they would have to accept responsibility for the global trade policies that have stolen our jobs and deflated our wages.

We must begin with the understanding that illegal immigration is a symptom of the disease that charades under the flag of Free Trade. We must begin by understanding that neither a wall nor mass deportation is a practical solution. The migrant workers who came to this country responded to the economic realities of their own nations – realities created by the global economic policies that our leaders in the White House and congress not only supported but sponsored.

We will fight for international labor laws, including the right to living wages, and the means to enforce them. We will fight against anti-labor laws in our own nation that falsely proclaim the "right to work" as they set up barriers to union organization.

In the case of China, a nation that parlays unfair trade, environmental recklessness and exploited workers to economic dominance, that owns our debt and possesses the means to control our currency, we recognize that we cannot reverse the damage that has been done over decades in a day, a year or even in four years but we must begin the reversal now.

In the cases of India, Malaysia, Indonesia, Latin

American and African nations, whose workers have been exploited to their ultimate detriment as well as ours, we should form a Fair Trade alliance to effect more immediate change, inviting the European Union and other nations to form a united front against the Free Trade mandate of the World Trade Organization, the International Monetary Fund and the World Bank.

On the issue of climate change and environmental protection, we must recognize that time is short and will not wait for economic reform. In the last few decades we have witnessed an acceleration of global warming and natural catastrophes. We can no longer afford to debate the relative responsibility of human causes; we must act now.

Recognizing that we have done more than any other nation and probably more than all nations combined to fill the planet's atmosphere with toxic pollutants, we hold a disproportionate responsibility to lead a green revolution.

Unlike labor standards and living wages, we cannot take a gradual approach to this crisis. We cannot allow China, India or any other developing nations to pursue the same industrial path that we followed in the last century. We must therefore enable all nations to follow a new path, a path of clean energy, a path that utilizes all the planet's resources in solar, geothermal, wind and other renewable sources, a path that maximizes fuel efficiency, localized production and global mass transit.

We can lead this monumental effort by redirecting the resources we have devoted to weapons of mass destruction and war or watch other nations lead while our economy continues to struggle against the tide of planetary evolution. We can lead by moving the world away from the growing threat and inevitable catastrophe of nuclear energy. As recent history has instructed us, nuclear energy begets nuclear weapons. We can afford neither and we must take the lead in disarming and dismantling both with dedicated and sincere resolve.

While we lead the world in this critical transformation, we cannot ignore the degradation of human values that has eroded our standing abroad even as it has weakened us at home. Liberty and justice can no longer be slogans for military invasion even as the rights of citizens are sacrificed at home to the false gods of patriotism and security.

On this there can be no compromise. The right to privacy in one's property, communications and personal affairs must be guarded religiously. The right to dissent in words and actions must be upheld. Freedom of religion, freedom of thought, freedom of speech and the right to assemble in protest must be defended. The Patriot Act must be exposed for what it is: A pretext for enabling the most abusive government intrusion into the private lives of its citizens in all of human history.

We believe in a press that cannot be bought and will not be used as a government propaganda agent. We believe that every media outlet has a solemn responsibility to investigate and report the facts without fear of consequence. We believe that media reform ensuring the independence and diversity of the press is essential to a functioning democracy.

We believe in the right of individuals to be free from government invasion and interference in all cases except where a clear and compelling cause can be demonstrated to an impartial judicial authority.

We have not thrived as a nation by backtracking on

the fundamental rights of our founding. Instead, we have always struggled to expand our rights and liberties and to defend them against the inevitable assault of our enemies.

At this critical time in our history, we must recognize that once again our most dangerous enemies are not those who would strike us from afar but those who live within our borders. These enemies wear the masks of our defenders. They have won positions of power and influence and they have launched a determined attack at the core of our greatness.

These enemies are not new to the American story. They were the profiteers and British loyalist during the revolution. They were the authors of the Alien and Sedition Acts. They were the traders and plantation masters who went to war rather than yield a way of life built on the exploitation of slaves. They were the corporate monopolists that suppressed labor with hired thugs. They were the McCarthy era fear mongers forcing citizens of every stripe to sign loyalty oaths and blacklisting those who resisted. They were the white supremacists preaching a gospel of intolerance, spreading terror with lynching and imposing their will with laws of segregation and disenfranchisement. They were the traditionalists who fought back women's suffrage and continue to fight women's rights and civil rights and opportunity for the least privileged among us.

The enemies of American freedom have always lived within our borders, disguised as friends and neighbors, waiting for the opportunity to press their cause of oppression. They always claim the moral high ground, always wear the badge of patriotism and always proclaim themselves defenders of the American way.

The enemies of America have come out of the shadows once again and it is the duty of every loyal citizen to oppose them with all the resolve and unity that we would summon to oppose a foreign invader.

We are at a crossroads. Perhaps all generations believe that theirs is the greatest challenge and all are largely correct. For as long as more and greater weapons are being developed without a reciprocal development of diplomacy and humanitarian values, the world of the future will always be more dangerous until at last the die is cast and we have crossed the threshold of no return.

I fear as we should all fear that we are approaching that threshold. That is the challenge we must embrace. That is the reason we will overcome all barriers to achieve a world that other generations have only dreamed: because we must, we will.

Jazz.

SPIES AMONG US

Eyes that Linger
Shadows in the Dark
Paranoia Paradox

Rome could not pinpoint the moment he first became aware of unfamiliar faces in familiar places, eyes that linger a moment too long, a soft click on the telephone, an overly eager volunteer, an inquisitive neighbor or an electrical worker with an interest in books and philosophy.

There are spies among us.

Things were going well on the political front though they were operating under the radar, supporting candidates in local elections that generally did not reveal party affiliation. Thanks to the mortgage crisis, they were buying storefronts at cut-rate prices in cities and communities across the nation.

The core policy group had come to a major decision. They would plot their course on a long-term trajectory. The storefronts were operating as community organizers for assisting the victims of a struggling economy. At a time when government services were decimated by budget cuts and administrators that believed in letting the chips fall, they would fill the void by renegotiating mortgages, bartering for goods and labor, setting up cooperatives and pooling transportation.

They were a self-sustaining organization, buying out foreclosed properties and converting them to affordable housing. When times were bad, as they were now, they would support the community. When times were good, the community would support them.

They were building from the ground up and they decided to lend their support to the first African American candidate for president. They did so knowing that the Senator from Illinois, though better than most, would still be confined by the money interests that control both parties. They did so not as a concession to the dominant party system but as a means to an end. They would help Obama become president and he would help the Independent movement reach a growing number of young volunteers.

The decision was not an easy one. Charges and countercharges of corruption and betrayal were hurled across the backroom at the Monastery until Rome, the lines of his face drawn in restrained anger and frustration, rose and made his case.

We're in it for the long haul, he explained. *If the past has taught us anything at all, it is that change does come without a price. We're trying to break a stranglehold that has held American politics captive for two hundred and eight years. That kind of change won't happen in one election or two or three. It builds brick by brick, mortar by mortar, and its success ultimately depends on our ability to hand the torch to the next generation and theirs to do the same.*

They needed young activists and Obama appealed to the young.

They would not work as Democrats. They would

work under their own flag. The Obama campaign invited their engagement and they would take advantage. They would help to win him the presidency and when he failed to deliver what his young followers naively expected, they would offer an alternative.

It was then that Rome began to notice the strays, the shadows, the spies. The power brokers in Washington realized they were a force that could turn an election and that made them a target. He assumed they were under the employ of political operatives not affiliated with any official government agencies but he could not be sure.

It was partly for that reason and partly for circumstances not yet defined that he was meeting with an internet specialist who came highly recommended. Amy had used him to run down some confidential information on a client the government was threatening under the despotic terms of the Patriot Act.

In a back room of the Monastery that Rome often used a workspace, the sound of jazz sifting through stone halls, soothing his soul and opening passages of imagination in his overworked mind, the young man knocked at an open doorway and shuffled inside. Hardly noticing Rome behind his desk, he looked around for a place to sit and stroked his hair in exasperation. Rome studied him like a master might study a prospective maid or a butler – someone he would trust inside his castle, his home.

Rome retrieved a chair from the hallway and returned to his perch, resuming his examination of the young man as he folded his canvas briefcase on his lap and searched for clues to the meaning of existence on the thick walls of stone where once a monk practiced a life of prayer and piety.

Weary of waiting for some verbal acknowledgement, Rome introduced himself and shook hands across the desk. His name was Freddie Prader though he was known as The Worm and he was looking for employment in internet management. He was clearly bright and just as clearly socially inept. Judging from his constant movement, tapping and fidgeting, he was either naturally high strung or a devoted amphetamine user or both.

Freddie pulled a file from his case and handed it to Rome. In it there was a dossier on every member of the inner circle, including information that Rome himself was unaware of, a list of contacts dating back over a year and most critically a detailed account of who had recently tapped the movement's database.

He looked up into the face of a smiling young man, fully aware of how impressive the accomplishment was. Rome's system was protected by state-of-the-art security. Until now, he would not have believed that anyone could break it. Now, he was alarmed and the meeting took on a new dimension. If this young man was not an ally, he was an extremely powerful enemy.

How did you get this?

Hire me and I'll tell you, Freddie smiled.

Rome suddenly saw the worm inside him and waited until the smile soured and the nervous fidgeting returned. What kind of man was this? He needed to know. Was he a mercenary or an idealist? What had Amy seen in him that he had not yet revealed? He removed his reading glasses and shook the kid down with a stare.

You'll tell me now or live the rest of your life looking behind your back.

Freddie was visibly stunned. It was all he could do to hold himself steady, to restrain from bolting like a bullied child. He had neither experienced nor anticipated this kind of showdown. To his way of thinking, it was all just a game.

As soon as he could gather his bearings, he explained exactly how he had gathered the information in question. He had the usual hacker codes and something more: He had a tap that could sense other taps and trace them to their source.

Rome realized the threat was not with Freddie but the knowledge he possessed. He could not only trace a tap but he could tap the source. Hapless Freddie had no idea how dangerous that kind of knowledge was and it fell to Rome to seize it to make sure it did not end up in the wrong hands.

Rome hired him on the spot as the head of a new technology unit with a generous salary. He did not ask if anyone else knew of his accomplishment. It was a part of the hacker's creed to demonstrate innovations and he was certain Freddie was not immune to the glory that his achievement would bring. He gave instructions to hire everyone he knew and trusted. He explained in matter-of-fact terms that some would kill for what he knew and others would kill to keep it from falling into the hands of adversaries.

The gravity of circumstance was beginning to register on Freddie's face. He felt compelled to explain his political views and commitment to the cause they represented. Amy had recruited him based as much on his activism as on his technical genius.

They sat down to dinner at restaurant down the street and talked philosophy, politics, dreams and visions. Freddie was the grandson of Czech immigrants. He had studied history and the age of revolution, including the Velvet Revolution, the Prague Spring that his grandparents so often remembered. They had fled their country with a dream of democracy, freedom and justice. They believed in America and they handed that faith down to their children and grandchildren. They were distraught with what was happening to America now.

Freddie related the story his grandparents had told him about the day the Russian tanks rolled into Prague. Until then, hope was in the air. Until then, they believed that democracy would come to Czechoslovakia without bloodshed. Until then, they believed in the power of ideas that rose up from the people and spread from universities to cafes to hospitals to common laborers. They wondered what would happen if they refused to work, refused to pay taxes, refused conscription and refused to be governed?

Then the tanks rolled in, blood was spilt and the great repression began. They crushed the people in the streets, men, women and children, beat them down like rabid dogs and along with them they crushed their dreams.

Rome related the story of the French Communard, a democratic-socialist uprising that seized control of Paris for a brief period in 1871. They granted women the right to vote and workers the right to organize. They stood first against a Prussian imperialist army and then against their own oppressive government. Against the Army of Versailles they held their ground until a traitor opened the gates and let the enemy inside. They fought courageously against impossible odds until late May when one hundred and seventy four holdouts at Pere-Lachaise Cemetery were line up against a wall and executed.

In the end 30,000 were killed and thousands more exiled but on the ninth anniversary of that massacre, 25,000 brave souls marched to the wall in protest. Two months later an amnesty was declared.

They shared the silence of knowing and the strength of believing even when the weight of history bears down on you. Tears welled in the young man's eyes as Rome recalled the youthful volunteers, the café radicals, the artists and dissidents who went to Spain and joined the International Brigades to fight against the fascists. *They were a ragtag group,* said Rome as if he were there, as if he was one of them, *fighting a well-trained army of professional soldiers with popguns and the spirit of solidarity.* Orwell and Hemmingway were among them. *Did they know it was a losing cause? How could they not? But it made them who they were. It shaped their vision of the world.*

Freddie sat a long time, studying the man before him, trying to understand what pushed him forward and what gave him hope. An evening fog was rolling in from the Strait of Juan de Fuca, winding through the Sound, comforting all souls with a cooling breeze. He emptied his glass of beer and leaned in to capture Rome's attention.

Is that what you want?

It was a familiar challenge and one that Rome had often invoked with his colleagues. Do you want to be a hero? In your heart, do you want to be the martyr shot down in the streets so that some future idealist will tell stories about you?

No, Rome answered. *I want to win.*

They shed tears for the International Brigades and the Communard of Paris and for centuries of struggle throughout history. They did not care whose ears were listening or whose eyes were hiding in the shadows. Rome was assured that Freddie could be trusted. He was a true believer and Rome was relieved. Had he not been trustworthy, Rome would have confronted a familiar dilemma: Doing wrong to do right was an inevitable confrontation in any cause or movement but it was not one to be relished.

He would not have to face that particular demon today.

They drank on a balcony overlooking the Sound until a yellow moon wavered and fell from the sky, raising toasts to Jefferson, Paine, Danton, Dubcek, Havel, Bolivar, Voltaire and Rousseau, and then they parted as brothers – or rather father and son – united in the cause of humankind.

Long Live the Revolution!

LAST REFUGE

Repentant Warrior
Volunteers for Exile
Wiping the Slate Clean

The decision by the Canadian Supreme Court not to provide refuge to the growing number of disaffected American soldiers was a crushing defeat. The nation that served as a safe haven for draft resisters in the Vietnam era served notice they will not play a similar role for those who misguidedly volunteered for the war on terrorism.

Sent to Iraq and Afghanistan they found themselves cast not as heroes and liberators but as villains, hated and despised by both sides in a civil war. With a judiciary tilted so far to the militant right it barely upheld the principle of habeas corpus - without which there would be no concept of justice save social and personal vengeance - what options were left to the soldier of conscience?

That was the question that Sara Kent asked of the nine justices as they denied refugee status to her client and scores of others. She vowed to press on with their cause in any way she could. She and a team of attorneys from both Canada and America were preparing a new case in the lower courts based on the widely acknowledged war crimes of American forces. Any nation that is a signatory to the Geneva Conventions, the International Criminal Court and the United Nations Charter is prohibited by statute from knowingly sending or returning an individual to a military force that would likely commit such crimes.

It was the kind of legal argument that Sara had grown to despise. Why not say what we mean and rest on the judgment of right and wrong? But that was not how the legal system worked. It required legalese and statutory analysis and case studies and real lives were in the balance. During the Vietnam War, Sara had helped many escape to Canada, which was then a willing refuge for all who suffered from conscientious awakening.

The first step was to put a roadblock in the way of Canadian deportation. As all legal processes, it required time and time was not something that all their clients had. For some they bought time. Others they referred to an underground organization.

The organization that Amy and Roy served was suddenly inundated with applicants for safe refuge. The vast majority of clients they had served were dissidents from countries where words alone were sufficient to risk loss of employment, detention, torture and death – consequences that were not confined to the individual but to their families and friends. They came mostly from war torn nations in Africa, Chechnya and the former Soviet Union nations, the Middle East and other nations lacking freedom of speech, freedom of belief and the principles of justice embodied in the Universal Declaration of Human Rights.

Amy and Roy ran a safe house where clients could be held until their papers were in order and arrangements were made for integration in another country. Host nations were generally aware of the organization's affairs and quietly approved but this was new territory. Until now their clients were intellectuals, professors and professionals that were welcome additions to most civilized nations.

American and coalition soldiers were another story. Most were unskilled workers and many came home from the war with deep emotional scars. Some would require long-term care, the kind of care America no longer believed in.

Miguel Estrada was such a man. Amy and Roy spent long hours talking to him, digging into his past, his experience in Iraq, his reasons for wanting out, the depth of his commitment to the cause: Was he willing to go to jail? Was he willing to start a new life in another country? Was he willing to give up contact with his own family for years if not a lifetime?

Miguel was not a simple man. He did not answer questions without fully understanding the meaning, without taking it in and pushing it around, like a new kid in the neighborhood, just to see what it was made of. His family worked in the fields of plenty in the southwestern states that for so many years welcomed his kind: the Mexican migrant labor force with roots both south and north of the border.

He spoke of the two nations in those terms: north and south. Both were America and both were more or less united states. As a child he believed in both. He had pride in both. He was grateful to the old country for taking care of his *familia*, for nurturing his parents and treating his grandparents with the kind of dignity that elders deserved. Grateful to his new country for welcoming him, for giving him an opportunity to experience higher education and for offering him a way to move forward, he wanted only to make a better life for himself and the family he expected to have.

As an adult he felt betrayed by both countries. He understood that both countries cared only for money. Corporate green he called it. Both exploited workers with substandard wages and working conditions. The south suppressed organized labor and the north, after enticing and using migrant workers, blamed them for everything that was wrong with their faltering economy.

Miguel understood little of this when he was forced to volunteer for service just before the September 11 attack. He served one tour in Afghanistan and two more in Iraq before he went AWOL.

He would not talk about what happened in the war beyond saying that he knew death from both sides. They sat in the living room of their Seattle home probing for more, tapping his emotions, watching the sweat build on the lines of his brow until they ran down his cheeks, joining his tears. They listened to his voice quiver and break as he struggled to release the demons that possessed him.

He would not go back. He would go underground. He would go to Guanajuato and disappear. He would go to jail but he would not go back.

Another evening of grinding, penetrating interrogation gave way to revelation. Amy looked at Roy and they both acknowledged a simple truth: they believed him. He was no longer a client; he was a friend. They would press him no further. They would search for the right answer to his dilemma.

Roy explained why it was necessary to treat him as they had but Miguel shrugged. He understood. You can't trust anyone or anything. A smile is not what it used to be. An outstretched hand may be the last you hold.

As a cool northern Pacific breeze filtered through an unseasonably warm Seattle evening, Miguel told a story of Marine revenge in a village outside Haditha. There was a report of collusion with the enemy, a safe haven where weapons and explosives were stored. Three homes were identified and his squadron was assigned to investigate.

Miguel bowed his head, closed his eyes and allowed his mind to retrieve the pictures, the sounds and senses he had fought so long to block out. His face revealed the terror he summoned from dark memories and his hands began to shake like an old alcoholic reaching for his last whiskey.

The others pressed him to lead. He was the most experienced. They pushed and prodded: Kill the kid. The rest will be easy.

He felt a charge of adrenaline that he mistook for the hand of justice, raised his pistol and sighted the boy's face. He saw his eyes widen and contract when disbelief gave way to the realization that the man before him was capable of such an act. They were dark eyes, prominent eyes, searching, seeking, and pleading eyes, the eyes of innocence, and the eyes of his people. They could have been his eyes or the eyes of his future son.

Amy's cell phone sounded Janis Joplin's *Ball and Chain* and the spell was broken. Miguel tried to resume his story, tried to retrieve the image, the crying, a mother's pleading in a foreign tongue, the smell of piss and fear, the sting of sweat in his swollen eyes, but he could not continue. He stammered and stopped, struggled and failed.

It was a place he could not go. It was a place that stripped him of his humanity, his dignity, his strength and confidence. He could not return there. Not now. Not again. He gasped for air like a marathon runner at the end of the race. Amy went to him, apologized again and again, cradled him until the waves of involuntary quivering released and gave him what comfort she could.

Roy, poised on a loveseat opposite them, every muscle in his body taut with the desire to act and knotted by the futility of that desire, watched and tried to put himself inside another man's soul. Was it even possible to imagine what he had seen? Was it even possible to imagine how he felt? The wound he carried was so much more penetrating than anything he was ever likely to experience that it left him breathless. How do you care for such a being? How do you treat that deep a wound?

And what of the child? Could he imagine the sight of the gun pointed at his head, the cries of his mother, the soldiers barking for blood vengeance? It was beyond imagining how he felt. Still, in the back of his mind, he knew he would write the story much as Miguel had told it, leaving the barrel of the gun hanging, balanced on the threshold of life and death, the eyes of a child inviting visions of a different path, a path of peace and mutual respect. It would fit well in a series of commentaries under the heading: The Untold Casualties of War. He would use an assumed name of course.

He shook himself to break free of the writer's mode. Amy had warned him, at quiet times of introspection when he was open to criticism, that it could make him seem aloof, as if he only cared in the abstract, as if he was observing real, breathing, sometimes bleeding human beings from a distance. Like a movie. It could make him seem insensitive, uncaring, cold…

At times like these Roy felt perfectly inadequate, an impotent being. His thoughts were pushed to the irrational conclusion: If only I can help this one… But for every one there were literally millions of others. The victims we are trained to care about like those of Iraq and Afghanistan and those we are conditioned to place beyond our emotions like the accursed of Myanmar, East Timor or the Congo.

They would do what they could and move on. It was a struggle with no end. They would do what they could do to help this man find refuge, a place to heal and begin again, and then they would move on to the next and the next and the next.

They waited until the convulsions of raw emotion subsided before explaining the options they could provide. They could give him a new identity and set him up in any major city in America other than San Diego where he last resided. He could move to Europe – London, Paris, Madrid, Barcelona – or Latin America – Caracas, Buenos Aires or Mexico City. Whatever he decided, wherever he went, he could not contact family or friends for at least two years.

Miguel took a deep breath and asked for time to think. It was a quiet night filled with agony and reflection. In his own way, he was freeing his mind of everything and everyone that bound him to his life. In the morning over coffee he told them he wanted to move to Chicago.

As a university student, he took a trip there once. If he had to start over at least he would begin with pleasant memories. It was place a man could lose himself in the crowd. It was a place where people had open minds and good schools. He wanted to resume his education. He wanted to become a teacher or a social worker. He wanted to help people like himself.

Amy and Roy nodded in agreement and promised to do everything in their power to make it so.

POLITICS IS LOCAL

The Neighborhood Terrorist
Hiding behind Badges
Words that Burn

In the tradition of Tom Paine, Jean Paul Marat and the Anarchists of Chicago, every movement has its pamphleteers and the Independence Movement had Roy Jones whose regular column appeared under the name of The Advocate. Everywhere a community activist center was established, its hub was a printing operation that turned out a weekly rag, featuring local issues and commentaries on national and international affairs, as well as posters and handouts for special events.

In a former age, the printing press was considered a weapon and it often fulfilled expectations. When a pamphleteer was accused of libel or treason, the publisher and printer were first in line of retribution. The press itself was a large cumbersome and expensive piece of machinery that could not readily be replaced if an angry mob was inspired by the local authorities or a competing interest to destroy it.

With the advent of the computer age, the press was no longer necessary. Now the danger was less from an angry mob than it was from the web. A skilled hacker in a remote location could take down an entire operation.

In Chicago, a city renowned for corruption and brutal repression of civil dissent, the Independent Center was established in the poverty-stricken neighborhood on the west side where once the Freedom Movement of Martin Luther King Jr., James Bevel and Bernard LaFayette centered its campaign to end slums and segregated housing in the city. In the days of the civil rights movement, they went to battle with a duplicitous Mayor Richard Daley who condescended in public while privately opposing their efforts and despising their leaders for the threat they posed to established order.

The Center was an abandoned storefront with glass doors and windows on the front where people on the street looked in to find volunteers shuffling papers, working on computers and counseling citizens in a flurry of activity. Organized chaos was the order of the day. There were two large desks, a couch and upholstered chairs around a large coffee table stacked with pamphlets, magazines and newspapers. The walls were covered with bookshelves filled with books. In the back there was an expansive room that housed the printing operation, a conference table and a podium with a few dozen folding chairs.

It was Friday evening and several volunteers were setting up chairs, putting up posters and laying out books and materials in preparation for a guest of honor. Roy Jones was coming to Chicago. He was virtually unknown to the greater community but within the circles surrounding the Center he was respected as the author of The Advocate.

He was coming to observe their operation, offer

advice and encouragement, address their concerns and talk politics. He had other contacts as well but this was his official business. The movement was already becoming restless and discontent with the rightward course of the Democratic nominee. The older activists had seen it all before and were neither surprised nor shaken by it. Democrat or Republican, a candidate tacked to the base during the primaries and worked back to center as soon as he secured the nomination. The younger activists however were disturbed by how stark and dramatic the transformation was from antiwar progressive to hawkish moderate.

Roy found it disturbing as well but he had a job to do. The message from the Independent Movement was clear: The movement needed Obama more than Obama needed the movement. There would come a time to rise up in protest if he failed to uphold their fundamental principles but that time had not yet come.

Strictly speaking it was not a right-center-left paradigm that described Obama's transformation. His backing of the FISA compromise allowing unwarranted surveillance on American citizens with minimal judicial oversight and immunity for the telecom corporations that allowed it was a betrayal of the libertarian right. His perceived backtracking on the war and foreign policy aggression, caving to the interests of the Israeli lobby among others, was neither a right nor left issue. There was nothing in either philosophy that justified acts of military aggression in violation of international law unless you considered it a massive unfunded government expenditure, in which case it was another betrayal of the fiscal conservative philosophy.

Moreover, if you considered where the majority of Americans stood on the issues then the center was where media described as the left: Complete withdrawal from Iraq on a timely basis, no more wars of aggression or wars for oil, an end to the policies of Free Trade and corporate deregulation, proportionate taxation on the elite to pay for health care and infrastructure, taxes on the oil companies to pay for alternative fuels, on and on.

Roy went through the list if only to demonstrate he understood their frustration; he in fact lived with it. His audience, a dedicated group of hardened local activists, a mixture of the old style radicals with worn jeans, unruly styles and ragged edges and a new younger appearing activist with more conventional styles, were attentive and respectful but doubt was written on their faces. More than half had supported Obama from early on in the campaign but now there were only a few left and they were quiet in their support.

He made the case that Obama was playing into their hands if they were smart. If not, they would play into Obama's. He was a far shrewder politician than he had been credited. The opposition had chosen to portray him as a typical liberal. They had handed him the crown of the most liberal Senator in Washington. It was an assertion that was absurd with the likes of Bernie Sanders, Barbara Boxer, Ted Kennedy, John Kerry and Russ Feingold in the Senate. So Obama countered by using such issues as FISA reform, gun control, free trade and an aggressive posture toward Israel's enemies in the Middle East to belittle the assertion.

Given Obama's strategy, attacks from the left worked to his advantage. It was up to the movement to show restraint. It was to their advantage to encourage the whisper campaign that he doesn't mean it. He is only doing what he has to do to win. He will end the war: Hang on to that. He will lead an energy revolution: Hang on to that. He will end corporate dominance of the political process.

It was to their advantage to criticize, yes, but always with a reminder that his opponent is far worse on every issue and the alternative is as yet nothing more than a symbolic protest.

He opened the floor to discussion and the attacks came like gunfire from an automatic weapon. How can I tell people what I don't believe without sacrificing my own integrity? Obama is just another politician. He threw us under the bus faster than Reverend Wright! Somebody tell me how he's better than McCain! He's the same old sell out! He won't end the war! He won't end the occupation! He'll expand the war to Iran and Syria or let Israel do it for us! The corporations own him! How can he change anything?

Slow down! I understand your complaints. At another time and place, I'd be standing beside you yelling at me! Just slow down and take it one step at a time: First, McCain is worse than Obama. He has one reason and one reason only for wanting to be president: To prosecute the war on terror. He believes we should have won in Vietnam and he wants his revenge. He has triangulated on every issue from abortion and torture to campaign finance and immigration. He will say anything to anyone if he believes it will allow him to get hold of the nuclear trigger. And if there's anyone here who doesn't believe he will use it, stand up and explain it to me.

A silence allowed a cold reality to set in. These people had always fought back at the notion of a lesser evil but they could not deny that Obama was by far the lesser of these evils. Every man and woman among them despised and feared McCain. Roy continued.

Second, this is not unexpected. We all knew Obama would cave on any number of issues. We knew he was a part of the system and therefore could not be a part of the change we need. The only surprise is how swiftly he accomplished it. What does that mean? It means he wants us to come after him. He wants us to prove to the American electorate that he is not one of us. He is not a radical. He is not a socialist. He is not a dangerous American with extreme beliefs.

Let's not give him what he wants. Let's go along. I'm not asking any of you to lie or deceive or mislead people in any way. Tell the truth but let that truth be Obama's time has come. We can't win the White House – not this time – but we can build a movement. You want to vote for Nader, fine. Ask him to open up his financing. Ask him why he never ran for an office he could win. A Senator or Governor Nader would have been a viable candidate. Jesse Ventura did it. Why not Nader? You want to vote for McKinney or Bill Barr, fine. Go work for them. Go with our blessings. We've been down that road before and we ain't going there no more.

It's simple: You work for the Independent Movement, you work for Obama. When the time comes and he knows it will, we break from him and we take a lot of his supporters with us.

A dark cloud lifted and everyone in the room remembered what it was that led them to join the movement. They were tired of the symbolic gestures, the hard fought campaigns to reach a threshold of five percent of the electorate, fighting windmills and slaying imaginary dragons, fighting back accusations of working for the enemy and pleas of holier-than-thou innocence.

They joined the Independent Movement because they wanted to work for real change. They joined for the long term. They joined to help create a viable political organization that was unafraid of compromise and getting dirty.

It was the same everywhere, a sense of betrayal, massive discontent. The central committee was working overtime to calm frayed nerves, sending representatives preaching the same message: Obama was not an end but a means to an end. Almost everywhere they received the message well. They needed to vent their outrage but in the end they moved beyond the crisis of the day.

They broke out a couple of cases of beer and sat around talking in more or less civil tones when suddenly the sound of shattered glass turned all heads to the street. When they opened the door the room began filling with smoke.

"Don't panic!" someone yelled as she opened a rear door and they all filed into the back alley where a couple of dark figures moved to a waiting vehicle and sped away.

They were lucky as it turned out. They had only recently cleared out the back room enough to clear the way for the rear exit. A week earlier they would have been trapped.

The police arrived an hour later and filled out a report with little interest. Even though almost all of them were locals, they were regarded as outsiders and they were on their own.

When Roy reported to Seattle he learned that similar events had taken place in five cities on the same evening. No one was seriously hurt. Clearly, someone was sending a message and security measures would have to be taken.

The following day stories appeared below the fold

in each of the local papers, detailing the event and quoting local officials questioning the nature of the organization. This kind of radical group attracts terrorist types and often leads to violence, they said. It was an orchestrated effort to discredit them with local and national connections.

The Movement counterattacked with press conferences explaining their grassroots commitment to democratic change and detailing the public services they had aided or provided without taxpayer support. They emphasized their abhorrence of violence and asked only that the local police force provide the same kind of protection that anyone else in the community received.

In the short run, the attack backfired. Volunteers came in by the dozens, offering assistance and contributions. Retired and off-duty police officers even offered to provide security. The movement was building community support.

The question remained: Who was behind it and what were their motives?

DARK SESSIONS

Stashing Bullets
Fire with Fire, Stone for Stone
Insurance Policies

Only in America could a cross dressing, power hungry freak who never married and savored the company of men become a singular institution that survived and in many ways transcended eight presidencies. If ever a man was beyond reproach, his name was J. Edgar Hoover, a name that stains the façade of the Federal Bureau of Investigation to this day.

From 1935 to 1972, as America was becoming the most powerful nation on earth, the most powerful man in the nation was J. Edgar Hoover. He had a dossier on everyone and everything that moved – especially anything within throwing distance to the halls of power in Washington D.C. Hoover famously underestimated the importance of organized crime while devoting unlimited resources to investigating such dangerous characters as Martin Luther King Jr. and John Lennon. Hoover played a critical role in the McCarthy era witch hunts and the Kennedy assassination whitewash.

John Sinclair was on the honor list of those who had

a file on record with the FBI when the agency was forced to release its records under the Freedom of Information Act. A highly redacted report suggested that Sinclair had flirted with radical ideologies and dangerous organizations but he always came back to the fold when it counted.

Sinclair learned a lot from J. Edgar Hoover. It was one thing to gather incriminating information; it was another to know how and when to use it.

The first time Sinclair met Roman Mason at a gathering of Seattle's political and social elite, he asked him how he made his money.

"The honest way," Rome replied to which Sinclair, without hesitation, said "Drugs?" Rome laughed. "Real Estate." Sinclair shrugged as if it was all the same. The Kennedy clan made theirs bootlegging during the Prohibition. JP Morgan, the Rockefellers, Dupont, Carnegie and Vanderbilt made theirs crushing small business, smashing organized labor and exploiting workers. Buy low, sell high, the law of the jungle: All the same.

They formed an immediate bond founded on cynicism. Rome struggled to transcend his but Sinclair embraced it. It gave him an edge. It guided his thinking. It led him to know long before the facts were in, who put the fix in and why. It enabled him to anticipate an enemy's moves.

Periodically, Sinclair and Rome convened special strategy sessions featuring the dark side of the political process. They were always closed on a need to know basis. Candidates and potential candidates, the public faces of the organization, were never invited. They need not know what they should not know so they would never have to hide uncomfortable facts.

On this occasion they were meeting at a café across the street from an old brick building where Freddie Prader had assembled a technology center on the top floor. It was late in the evening, a half moon high in the sky, a cool breeze breathing the scent and taste of the northern Pacific to the second-story balcony where Freddie sat opposite the old masters, John Sinclair and Rome Mason, a little in awe.

Freddie set out to explain the system but Sinclair cut him short: Just tell me what you know.

Sinclair had already postulated the source of the attacks. Freddie's reverse surveillance technology confirmed what Sinclair suspected: The Obama camp had come to the conclusion that their assistance was no longer required. The Independent Movement was needed when the nomination was in doubt but now they were perceived as a liability. Better to uproot the cause now before it grew and spread. Republican operatives were recruited to the cause making it a bipartisan mission to stamp out the little guys. The major parties always found cause for unity when it came to keeping the system closed. Of course, they were willing to play the game, Republicans supporting Ralph Nader, Democrats supporting Bill Barr, as long as there was no chance the independent would become viable.

Rome was surprised the betrayal came so soon. It was arrogant of the Obama people to think they had it in the bag already. There remained more than three months of campaigning before the election. Anything could happen and most often did.

If Obama himself approved or gave the order it could never be documented. The one thing the candidate had proven beyond doubt was that he was politically savvy. He was after all a Chicago politician. Layers of plausible deniability protected him. A dozen operatives were willing to fall on the sword to keep the new messiah safe. Still, he could be wounded by doubt and by being compelled to throw another trusted aide under the bus.

Sinclair assured Rome they had plenty of ammunition at their disposal and declared it time to give them a taste of their own dirt. Rome sensed he was holding something back (he was of course holding the Simon Juneau file) but decided it was not time to press.

He suggested releasing a series of speculative articles on the web, dropping names and citing dates and locations - things no one should know outside their circle. It would be enough to let both sides know they were not playing with amateurs. Attacks would be answered in kind. Blood for blood.

Freddie nearly dropped his beer and groped for an I Pod device in his jacket pocket. Something was happening. He looked across the street where the dim lights of security monitors and exit signs, lights that never went off, suddenly did.

Rome caught his gaze and sensed the panic behind them. "Let's go," he said standing, even before four men in dark suits emerged from a white SUV, jimmied the lock in a matter of seconds and went inside. Rome tossed a couple of bills on the table and went for the door with Sinclair and Freddie following. They walked down the stairs toward the glass doors that opened to the street when Freddie pleaded with them to wait. He had access to the monitors on his device and informed them that one of the men was stationed outside as a lookout.

They went to the back of the building where they found an emergency exit wired for security.

Sinclair: *Can you fix it?*

Freddie with a laugh: *I'm a tech wizard, not an electrician.*

He studied the small screen of his device as if he were a baseball fan watching the ninth inning of a World Series game.

Rome: *Can you see them?*

Freddie nodded. He had connected his entire security system to the device in his hands.

Rome: *Can you hear them?*

Freddie flipped on the volume and allowed them to listen and observe. They stood in a storage area with boxes, maintenance supplies and a row of folding chairs against a wall. Sinclair pulled out three chairs and they sat down, listening and waiting.

Is it recording? Yes.

Wind it back to where they first entered the center.

Freddie did so and they watched three of the men break in, one taking the lead with a gun, securing the premises, another walked directly to a computer station and began tapping on the keyboard while the third hung back until he received the "all clear." He called a number on his cell phone, reporting that the target was secured but no one was home. He seemed disappointed.

"That's enough," said Rome. Freddie nodded and went back to monitoring the situation live. One man stood at a window with binoculars, scanning the street. Another still pounded away at the keyboard and the third, the boss man, looked over his shoulder.

Freddie: *He'll never crack it.*

Rome to Sinclair: *Who are they?*

Sinclair with a shrug: *Professionals. Government trained but they could be anyone.*

Rome: *Let's find out.*

Rome dialed 911 on his own cell and reported a burglary in progress, hanging up just as Freddie reported some disturbing news.

Freddie: *Shit! Shit! They've spotted your car. The lookout is walking across the street to check it out.*

The three men on folding chairs were starting to sweat, watching the little screen where a man shined his flashlight inside the car. He checked the door, looked up at the lights from the café and smiled.

Rome to Freddie: *Where are you parked?*

Parking lot down the street.

Sinclair: *What do we do now?*

Rome: *We wait. If we get a break, we make it to Freddie's car and get as far away from here as we can.*

If we don't?

Rome shrugged. Either way they would find out what was going on.

Freddie: *He's headed this way.*

The brief squawk and beating blue light of a patrol car announced its presence and pulled up across the street. The man stopped, sighed, and walked over to the squad car. They could not make out what was being said outside the building. He seemed to be trying to explain the situation but the officer did not buy his story. He pulled his gun, disarmed the man, cuffed him and deposited him in the back of the squad car. He then examined the broken doorway and entered the building on alert.

Sinclair: *That's our break.*

They walked out the front door, past a frustrated man in the back of a squad car shaking his head, to

Freddie's VW van down the street. They piled in without a word and Freddie began driving before he realized there was nowhere to go. He took a left turn, then a right and parked at an all night bar, where the three of them observed the proceedings back at the technology center.

After an initial flurry of shouts, hands up and against the wall, the boss man produced an identification that settled the dispute.

In a muffled voice he said: *Homeland Security.*

Like the Gestapo in Nazi Germany, Homeland Security was all he needed to say. No one questioned it and no authority or individual was allowed to protest against it. Well, there emerged from the cracks a whimper here and there but what did it accomplish? If you protested long and loud enough, you got your name put on a list. If your name came up again, they took you away.

Like the Reign of Terror, the Spanish Inquisition or the French Gendarme in Algiers, the process was self-sustaining. Who was the enemy? They were on the list. How did they get on the list? They asked too many questions. They said yes when they should have said no. They said no when they should have said yes.

It was easy. It was too easy.

Rome: *What do you think, John?*

Sinclair: *If it were my operation, I'd round them all up in one sweep. Not the locals, the volunteers, but the core.*

Three men sat in an old VW van, two old and one young, lost in the world and searching for their next move. Their pasts erased, their bank accounts wiped clean, they were no longer whom they were. They were nonentities. They were aliens in their own land.

Freddie: *Shit. What do we do now?*

A PATRIOT DIRGE

Rome: *Well, I have a cabin off the books and off the grid, up on the north coast of the Sound. No phone, electricity on a generator. They'll find it but it will take a while, maybe a week. After that we have two choices: Canada or Mexico and Canada is a lot closer.*

Freddie: *Shit.*

Rome: *You ready for this, John?*

The old man smiled, sincere and heartfelt, memories of past battles racing through his mind, the taste of blood fresh on his lips.

I was born ready for this.

Freddie kicked it in gear and they drove north into a moonlit Seattle night as their thoughts raced in all directions at once. Contingencies. Contingencies. All roads blocked, all paths uncertain. So be it. They were born for this fight.

THE SIEGE

Port Townsend Retreat
Hunter and Hunted
Covering Tracks

Roy was worried but it did not matter. Amy was in a mood for celebration. Miguel Estrada was safely implanted in his own apartment in Chicago. He had a job at a local market and was enrolled in night classes at the university.

Even the recent spate of attacks on neighborhood activist centers did not alarm Amy. It was a sign the opposition, the parties in power and the hands that guided them, were concerned. They were a threat and they were making an impact. That it happened so soon was surprising but it was inevitable. They were prepared. They would hold their ground and strike back.

Roy was convinced it went beyond party politics. He was convinced it was the first volley, a shot across the bow, a warning before an all-out assault on the organization. He had to admit, as a writer, he was prone to exaggeration, even bouts of paranoia, so it was easy to discount his own fears and yield to Amy's optimism.

They booked a hotel in Port Townsend, took a ferry

across the Sound and spent the day wandering from shop to shop, sipping lattes, enjoying good food and spirits, sitting in the sun and listening to an open-air blues festival. Port Townsend was a place of artists, poets, musicians and intellectuals, people who understood the way the world worked and fought to make it better.

It was a place of beauty that collected people like Roy and Amy, whose idealism was sown in the cultural tapestry, a mélange of unique individuals connected by common values and a collective vision of utopia. A dancing girl smiles at strangers. A bearded man passes out free water. Solar panels on rooftops and hybrid vehicles. A spirit of acceptance, tolerance, appreciation and earthbound equilibrium. Here there was a sense of living and being in harmony with the planetary soul.

It was a sensation that neither Roy nor Amy had felt in a long time, not since the age of flower children, free love, counter culture and radical antiwar and anti capitalism sixties – or what modern historians called the sixties which was really the years between 1967 and 1972, a coming of age for a generation of revolutionaries. It was a long, long time ago, longer even than the years that marked its passing. But in this place, with the lush green mountain forest of Olympic Peninsula behind them and the majestic currents of the Sound before them, it was easy to remember.

They breathed the cool oceanic air, forgot their plots and plans, their worries and frustrations, and rediscovered youth in each other's arms.

Sitting on a balcony in the late evening, watching the ferries roll in and out, Roy felt a rise in passion and Amy caught the wave. They returned to their hotel room and made love with the vigor of youth and the knowledge of age. She teased him with her pointed breasts, chided him for his impatience, and drove him to the edge of madness before the final act.

Breathless, they lay entwined, arms and legs, in the scent and aura of desire.

Amy suddenly had an unbearable hunger for ice cream, Ben and Jerry's Whirled Peace and Cookie Dough. He knew better than to question it.

She threw on some clothes and blew him a kiss on her way out.

"Be back in ten minutes."

It took longer than ten minutes. The place she had in mind was no longer in business. It seemed not even Port Townsend was immune to a growing recession. She drove on until she found an all-night market, enjoyed a conversation with the clerk and climbed back in the car for the return drive when she got a text message on her cell.

"Code Blue," it read. "Take cover."

She was baffled. There was no Code Blue – not that she was aware of – and she did not recognize the source. A knot was building in her stomach as she drove back to the hotel. Roy's paranoia was taking hold and she could not wash it away.

What's happening? Was he right? Is this the beginning of a siege? Who were they and how far were they willing to go?

She shook her head and told herself it was nothing, just a joke or a prank, but her brow was suddenly warm and she could feel beads of sweat rolling down to join tears building in her eyes. She told herself it was nothing, a false alarm, something they would laugh about, but she was scared and wanted only to get back to the hotel.

She pulled over half a block short when she noticed a white van parked in front of the hotel. She looked up at their room and the curtains were drawn. She drove slowly down the road, spotting a man in a suit at the entryway, looking around.

Did he see me? No. Maybe. I don't think so.

She parked around the block, got out and eased up to the corner of a building where she could see the front of the hotel. Another man in a suit appeared and exchanged words with the man on lookout. They seemed concerned and looked around. Finally, two more men emerged with Roy in cuffs. They threw him in back of the van as a couple just entering the hotel looked on in astonishment.

For a moment she was paralyzed. She understood what was happening but she could not accept it. She could not escape the feeling that it was her fault. He knew what was happening.

We should have taken precautions.

She also knew they would be looking for her now. She bit down on her lip and allowed the survival instinct that had served her so many years and guided her through so many difficult situations, to kick in.

She moved back to the car with the silence of a cat, climbed in and waited for the van to pass in front of her. Then she turned around and drove.

Certain they would be looking for her at the landing, not certain if any ferries ran this late at night, she headed south and drove into the night. She steeled her nerves for planning her next moves: Drive to Tacoma, cut over to the interstate and up to a safe house in Seattle. It was an empty apartment designed for this occasion: high security internet access, low profile, a spare car registered in Canada, a gun, cameras, cell phones and a printer designed to reproduce authentic altered identification.

She planned no further. At the safe house she would find out what went down, who was swept up in the siege, who was holding them where and the charges drawn against them. She sensed what she was up against and recoiled. She was sickened that Roy was caught and not her. Caught? They were not criminals. *Unless participating in the political process is criminal activity, they were no different than any other common citizen.*

Sara felt the heat rising and let it go. Who were these people? What entitled them to trample on the Bill of Rights? From what well did this authority spring? Centuries of progress, liberty and justice, undone in less than a decade – and to do so in the name of democracy! The arrogance of power and the audacity of kings!

At this moment she understood the mindset of a terrorist. At this moment, she knew how a woman could strap explosives to her body and blow herself up. At this moment, if there were a magic button that could blow up the White House, she would have pressed it.

But they had broken the law, hadn't they? They helped illegal immigrants and deserters escape the hand of justice in the name of justice. They did not agree with the law but they could not reach out to the law for help. They worked outside the law, in the cracks where justice fell through, but they knew the potential consequences.

They knew the risk but everything she felt, everything she had learned, everything she witnessed and experienced in the world told her to resist. It was the duty of every citizen to resist in every way they could. That was the lesson of the founders. That was the culmination of knowledge from generations of dissent.

The Bill of Rights was enshrined in the universal law that governed all women and men not for the mindless masses and not for the elite but for those who chose to oppose a government that regarded its people as a shepherd regards his sheep.

They would not get away with it. They would pay a price. The movement would not go down in silence. Too much was at stake.

Sara fought the urge to press down on the gas pedal. She fought to regain control. If they were going to strike back, if they were going to prevail, a cool mind and a steady hand was worth a thousand clenched fists. This was her calling. This was her battle. It was the fight she had waited for her entire adult life.

Like the Freedom Train abolitionists, like the French underground, like the Warsaw resisters, like the student protesters of Kent and Jackson State, like the Civil Rights activists in Mississippi and Alabama, like the farm workers in the Cesar Chavez army, like the suffragettes and the lonely figure who stood before the tanks at Tiananmen Square, like the Buddhist priest who set himself aflame in protest of Vietnam, Amy was born to this cause, this moment, this destiny. She had no choice. Her only regret was that Roy was no longer at her side to help shoulder the burden. Maybe that was their destiny and his: to be held at an anonymous detention center, hauled before a secret tribunal, to be interrogated and to resist. It was not what they wanted but it was the hand they were dealt.

She drove into the night, letting down her windows to take in the crisp cool air. It was a pleasant night in

Seattle. Most of the people were comfortable in their quiet homes, sleeping in their soft beds. How few of them knew the world had changed.

All her tears spent, Sara drove through Seattle and made her way through quiet streets to the suburban apartment house where a bed and safety awaited. She parked her car in the garage and took the elevator to the apartment. A click of the key, a flick of the light...no one home.

Thank god.

She sat down at the computer and began to learn everything she could about what happened the night before.

FLASHBACK

The Enemy Wears No Uniforms
Sleep and Sleeplessness
Kill Me or Let Me Go

Miguel read somewhere that some tormented souls afflicted by seizures opted for lobotomy rather than suffer the consequences of their affliction. He wondered if there was a similar procedure for memories. When he asked an army doctor she told him there was – only it was less intrusive. She wrote a prescription. For the next six months he walked around in someone else's mind and body, not knowing who he was or what he would do next.

He threw the pills away to see if he could find some remnant of his soul, hiding deep within the shell of a soldier. He did but it was a sleepless soul. He no longer slept. He lay down, closed his eyes and eased the tension of his muscles but he did not sleep. In a war zone it was dangerous to take sleeping medication. You never knew when you might need all your senses at alert so he did not sleep.

He counted the days until his four-year term of enlistment expired only to discover that the government that signed him up would not honor it. Under a "stop loss" order from the commander-in-chief they could keep him as long as the needed, as long as they wanted and as long as the war went on.

Without sleep he had no nightmares. He had only memories and memories slowly faded. He still had flashbacks – unpredictable and infrequent but as vivid as the stars on a clear night in the Rockies. Triggered by strange sensations, the smell of kerosene, the pop of a worn light bulb, a shadow on a dark wall, an unfamiliar accent, the crushed shell of a vehicle or burning oil, they came and went like ghosts at a cemetery.

He slept without sleeping with a loaded gun under his pillow until he almost shot a friend with whom he was staying.

Now, six weeks after he went AWOL and four days since settling in to his Chicago apartment, Miguel Estrada was beginning to believe that the nightmares and flashbacks were finally behind him.

He had a routine and he clung to it like a preschooler to a teacher's praise. Six o'clock rise, pack a lunch, toast and coffee, report to work, grocery shopping and a quiet evening at home. He watched the evening news, caught a movie and retired with a tattered copy of Gabriel Garcia Marquez' *One Hundred Years of Solitude* between ten and ten thirty. He always set the alarm though he was certain it was not necessary.

He would begin night classes at the University of Chicago in five more weeks, when the sultry days of summer gave way to the chill winds of autumn. Then, he would set a new schedule and begin again.

Someday, he told himself, *I'll go out and paint the town*. It was his last conscious thought every night and this night was little different. He pulled a pillow under his head, closed his eyes and let his mind drift where it would. Tonight it drifted back to Iraq, back to Tikrit and back to an Iraqi child pleading for help, pleading for mercy, begging for his mother's life, his father already dead, his brothers and sisters behind his mother's skirt.

He sprang from his bed when he heard the sound of a door opening. His vision clouded, his head a jumble of fear and loathing, sweat flowing from his pores though it was not warm in his air-conditioned apartment, he was no longer in Chicago.

He was back in Iraq where the enemy wears no uniform. The soft sound of footsteps, click of a gun and he went for his but came up empty. Standing to face the enemy, he felt a blast on his chest that pushed him against the wall, a lamp crashing to the floor.

His vision cleared and he could see that the men before him were not Iraqis. They were not soldiers either though they conducted themselves as soldiers would. They were yelling at him not to move and to hold his hands up. He did so and they moved in, patting him down though he was wearing only his underwear, and binding his wrists in cuffs.

"Who are you?" he asked.

"Homeland Security," one man replied.

"Is this America?" he asked.

The man laughed. Yes, but not the America you know and love.

"Why am I being arrested?"

"We'll tell you all about it," he said.

When they searched the room, they allowed him to dress. Then they hauled him down to a waiting van and took him to a local detention center. It was a building downtown, hiding in plain view, without windows and with no visible signs of what it contained inside.

Ever been arrested before, Mr. Estrada? Miguel stared at the wall behind the interrogator. He was a soldier in enemy hands. He had his training to fall back on. *We know you have. This country gave you a second chance, a chance to start all over, and how do you repay us? No, I wouldn't have much to say either. But we're a forgiving country. We're going to give you another chance. Give us what we want and we let you walk. That's right: A free man, a citizen of these United States. His obligations and debts to this great nation paid in full. What do you think of that?*

It was a small room with white walls, a white ceiling, cement floor and a wall of observation mirrors. Miguel stared at the wall, searching for another place and time where no one could reach him, and the interrogator turned to the man standing behind him.

We offer the deal of the century and what does he do? Stares into space like a dumb wetback. Yeah, we know who you are and we know what you've done.

They took him to a padded room, all white, his wrists and ankles bound. Light so bright he could hardly see. One wall had a screen and the other a projector. For the next twenty-four hours they played highlights from the war in vivid color, featuring scenes from Fallujah, Tikrit, Haditha and Guantanamo Bay.

It was as if there was a camera over his left shoulder in Iraq, the volume so high it rattled his brain. They fed him a green semi-liquid mixture with no discernable taste and a plastic spoon. They watched him, filmed him and fed back his sorry image superimposed on the war.

Ever heard of rendition, private? Ever heard of flagging?

We could send you back, you know? We could send you to one of our friendly allies…or not so friendly. They'd love to get their hands on you.

"I want a lawyer."

Haven't you heard? Terrorists don't get lawyers. No rights, no due process, no habeas corpus. You belong to us.

After three days of the same routine and several injections resulting in hallucinations he began to crack. His interrogators smelled weakness in the rank odor that radiated from his skin. They pressed harder.

You can put an end to this right now. A signature on the dotted line and you can go home.

Something about his smile, his audacity, his air of victory suddenly sparked Miguel's indignation. He returned to his silent resistance for three more days.

All right, Miguel, you've proved your point. You're a tough guy. We'll give you that. But now it's time to play ball.

Balled up in the corner of his padded cell, Miguel turned his head only slightly and began to take in even, heavy breaths of air.

"Kill me."

What's that?

"Kill me or let me go."

The interrogator laughed but a sigh betrayed his frustration. He was beginning to wonder if they were wasting their time.

Cruelty and inhumanity bordering on torture was not an easy job for a man who had not yet given up on the guiding principles of democracy. No matter how it was rationalized, each act at variance with his internal code of conduct tore at his gut and stole hours of peaceful sleep.

He gave his colleague a grim assessment.

Better contact the agency. We've gone as far as we can go.

THE HIDEOUT

Taking Stock
Prisoners in a Free Land
Escaping the Hand of Injustice

As Rome knew too well, living too long in a confined space can drive one mad. Living with others in a confined space raises tempers, pushes patience to the tipping point and tests even the strongest relationships. When Amy joined Sinclair, Freddie and Rome at his one room cabin on the north coast of the Sound, Sinclair was reminded of Jean Paul Sartre's *No Exit:* Hell is other people.

If not for the urgency of the situation and their unity of purpose, something would surely have exploded. Freddie resented that he was the designated gopher for supplies but he was a logical choice as Sinclair pointed out for he was essentially nondescript, a common type in this part of the country. Freddie argued that he had far more important things to do, having adapted Rome's rudimentary technology into a secure, working system. It was undeniably true but it was also true that Sinclair, Rome and Amy were too recognizable to be seen in public.

Amy took the chance of contacting Rome by email and Freddie picked it up. After some discussion they forwarded instructions to rendezvous at a supermarket parking lot in Bellingham. It was a thirty-mile drive for Freddie who grumbled every minute going and coming.

The circle was closing and there little time to waste. Between Amy and Freddie, they pieced together what had happened and who was caught in the round up. In keeping with the administration's notorious ineffectiveness, only Roy and Miguel had been detained, held by Homeland Security at unknown locations. The only item that appeared in public media was a small article in the Washington Post suggesting that Representative Maggie Thomas was under investigation on unspecified conspiracy charges. It appeared Maggie was being threatened in exchange for her silence. Sara Kent in Canada was beyond their reach unless they could come up with more substantial charges.

The Independent Movement was the sole target of the operation. Miguel Estrada had the misfortune of being there with Amy and Roy while they were under surveillance. When they found out about his desertion, his semi-criminal record and immigration status, they decided he could be used to turn evidence – real or concocted – on the others.

Roy knew better than to resist the inevitable interrogations. His instructions were to wait twenty-four hours and then tell everything he knew. By then, the organization dedicated to providing safe refuge to dissenters and dissidents in all nations would have closed shop only to turn up elsewhere. Miguel had no such instructions. There was little need because he had little knowledge.

They sent out an encrypted message informing

everyone in the Independent Movement exactly what had occurred. It asked them not to act and to hold the information back until the next communication.

They all agreed that the next move was to get out of the country. Having provided that service to countless clients, Amy took care of the details: false identification, passports, vehicle registration, bank accounts and Canadian citizenship. They would take the obvious route on the interstate through Vancouver. A less populated border station would raise suspicion. The story (if they needed one) was that they were returning from a week of vacationing in Seattle. A hapless Freddie would pose as Amy's son.

They each packed a modest bag, loaded them in the trunk of Amy's Canadian Honda Civic, and headed north with Amy driving. Once they crossed the border, they would drop the façade, check into a prominent hotel under their own names and defy American authorities to act. They would apply for political asylum and stand their ground in court on the foundation of international law.

Apprised of the situation Sara Kent was in motion, making security arrangements, organizing a legal team, laying the groundwork for asylum, securing financing and informing a community of activists. Everything hinged on the four of them making it to Canadian soil. The Americans made a huge mistake failing to capture them. It was uncertain why they left Maggie out of it to this point but they might have waited until Sara was back in America where her dual citizenship could not protect her. It was as they said: If not for the gross incompetence of the Bush administration and its team of political lackeys, they might have succeeded in gutting the constitution and eviscerating what remains of American democracy. They might succeed in any case but their collective lack of foresight and inability to execute their malignant intent provided an opportunity for effective resistance.

The incompetence of the Neocons was rivaled by the ineffectiveness of the antiwar movement. The same movement that brought three million protestors to the streets only to see the war go on without a hitch now seemed hopelessly divided. United in opposition to the Iraq War, divided on the Afghan War, united in opposition to Bush and the Neocons but divided on supporting Obama. United on policy but divided on strategy. The path to political resistance was blocked at every turn. Little wonder both parties sought to crush a budding independence movement in its infancy. They had a stranglehold on power and the only thing that could interrupt their plans was a viable third choice. Ralph Nader was not a threat because he had no coattails and he refused to take the long road that would have given him the one quality he lacked: legitimacy.

It was the same cycle of helplessness to hopelessness that led Sara away from politics only to be drawn back by extremes of injustice and a ruthless disregard for the people of a kind formerly known only in military dictatorships. Now that she was back, she would fight the good fight with everything she had at her disposal.

As they turned onto the Interstate heading north, Amy's mind was racing through contingencies. She cautioned the others that once they got past the last exit in the states there was no turning back. Whatever happened they could not escape. They could only play the hand they were dealt. There was some discussion concerning logistics, the location of the last exit and the likelihood of their being discovered but they all agreed (with a mild objection from Freddie who thought he could make a run for it) that the best tack was to remain calm and stick to the story.

As they passed the turnoff to Ferndale approaching the border, Freddie's phone buzzed. The others nodded their approval and he answered it. A woman's voice identified herself as Aunt Sara and asked to speak to Freddie's mom. Baffled (he had no Aunt Sara), he handed the phone to Amy.

"Have you crossed the border yet?" the voice inquired. No, they had not.

"Good. There's a wonderful gift shop on Drayton Harbor. Northern Lights it's called. They have these fabulous statuettes of dolphins. Would you mind stopping there to pick one out for me?"

Amy identified the voice as Sara Kent. There was a problem. They were walking into a trap and they were being monitored as they spoke.

"I'd love to," she replied.

"Wonderful! Take the 275 Exit and follow the road south. It's right there on Drayton Harbor Road. You can't miss it."

"All right," said Amy. "We'll see you when we get there."

She took the exit and proceeded south at a snail's pace. She explained what was happening and everyone looked to Freddie who was suddenly flush and fidgeting even more than normal.

"Did you call someone before we left?" asked Rome.

"My mom," he replied, "but there's no way they could crack the code!"

"They cracked it," said Amy. "And now they're tracking us."

"Idiot!" added Sinclair.

Freddie felt like a kid caught in a lie. It was a lesson he was still learning: Confidence is no excuse for carelessness. He apologized and promised it would not happen again.

Another ten minutes and they would have been in the custody of Homeland Security. Sara got a tip from someone who knew someone in the border patrol who in turn knew to contact Sara. Two vans of special agents were waiting for them even now.

Amy pulled into a café parking lot on Drayton Harbor Road, pulled out a map and explained her thoughts: They could not go back to the cabin because that was where they began tracking them. They could go back to her Seattle safe house but they could not know how long it would remain safe. Alternatively, they could plant the phone in a vehicle heading south. She pointed to a pickup with Oregon plates. It would buy time while they headed east to the next border crossing.

"With any luck we'll be on Canadian soil in less than an hour."

Rome and Sinclair agreed. They would not turn back. Freddie remained silent as if he had lost the right to offer an opinion. He turned off his cell phone and stuffed it in a crack between a metal toolbox and the sideboard in the back of the pickup.

Rome was incensed. It was all he could do to hold it in check. Not at Freddie. Freddie made a fool's mistake. It came with youth. His rage was directed at the nation that gave him birth, nurtured him and gave him an opportunity for growth. He was enraged at the betrayal. He was enraged at the mendacity of a government that turned on its own citizens for engaging the political process. He was enraged that the men and women who captured the reigns of power by subterfuge and fraud could now brand those who stood in opposition traitors to the nation. He was no traitor. He was no criminal. He loved America. He loved its founding principles, its idealism, its hope and dream. He loved the spirit of the American people – hard working, stubborn and devoted to family. Anyone who judged Americans as egocentric or rugged individualists did not know Americans. More than anything in the world, Americans wanted to belong.

He shifted in his seat and gazed out the car window, his eyes unfocused, looking inward, holding back the rage.

Sinclair was more or less amused. He could think of nothing better than to spend the last days of his life on earth a fugitive from the law. This was a grand adventure, a journey with a purpose, and the prospect, however remote, of reaping revenge tasted sweet. He loved the movement, the smell of the pines, the crisp fresh air and the companionship of his fellow travelers. It seemed his entire life was painted in shades of gray but this was vivid, striking color. He was on the side of virtue and he savored it.

He was profoundly content and the smile that painted his lips struck the others as strange. They did not know his fate was just over the horizon. They could not know how grateful he was to be riding this remote road on a cool summer day.

They drove in relative silence, an occasional "idiot" emerging from Sinclair, until they came to the border crossing at Sumas. The border agent looked them over, asked the typical questions – any fruits or vegetables – and welcomed them home to Canada.

Somewhere around Tacoma a startled Oregonian was stopped and interrogated by agents of Homeland Security.

ROY'S HOLIDAY

A Time to Write
A Comfortable Incarceration
Room with a View

After twenty-four hours, Roy was free to answer all questions openly and candidly. It was standard procedure for the organization that Roy served alongside Amy to provide safe refuge to international dissidents. When the organization was founded it was inconceivable that they would be called to serve American citizens – or for that matter residents of the European Union. Everything changed the day the towers fell.

Caught and detained in a security sweep, Roy was prepared to provide names, identities, locations, timelines and events but his inquisitors did not seem interested. The intake interview was cursory:

Are you who we think you are? Yes, I am.

Where is Amy Goodall? Somewhere in the Seattle area.

Are you an associate in an organization known as the Independent Movement? Yes.

After twenty-four hours he confirmed what they already knew: that the Inner Circle of the Independent Movement consisted of six individuals, including himself, Amy, John Sinclair, Sara Kent, Representative Maggie Thomas and its founder Roman Mason. He told them that they were a political organization committed to change through the electoral process. He told them they were dedicated to the principles of nonviolence, including civil disobedience and mass protest.

Sitting across a dark wood desk in an expansive library, his interviewer dutifully took notes and read them back to confirm their contents. He identified himself as Agent Black and he maintained a decorum of polite but guarded respect. It was as if he knew it was all just a scam, that Roy was little more than a dupe and he himself was being used by opportunistic politicians for nefarious purposes.

Roy had the feeling that if Agent Black could speak freely he would say he deplored the individual who gave the order for this operation. He knew it was wrong. He knew it was an abuse of power but he was not in a position to question it.

For the record he made a point of opening every session with a request for an attorney. Agent Blake took note and moved on.

It did not feel like interrogation. It did not feel like imprisonment. They were in a large hotel-like structure in a remote forested location. His room was spacious, carpeted and finely furnished with rows of books and a writing desk. The windows were barred but he could see Mount Rainier in the distance.

It was more like a writer's retreat than an unlawful detention. He was allowed paper and pen. He could listen to music, watch television, even access the internet with a monitor at his side. The food was good, the wine more than decent. He could eat alone in his room or join the agents downstairs.

He soon discarded any notion of escape and got down to serious writing: Political articles chronicling the abuses of the current White House, the failure of the political process, betrayals of civil liberties and the separation of powers. Having long neglected his creative impulse, he began to write fiction as well, including a long short story about a political purge not unlike what had befallen the Independent Movement. Agent Black read his work on a semi-regular basis. Their sessions were evolving into literary reviews.

"Is that what happened?" the agent asked.

"You know the facts," responded Roy. "You tell me."

They were so accommodating that Roy began to wonder who was pulling the strings. These were serious people, sincere and dedicated. They did not enjoy wasting their time on a political junket. They were being used and they knew it. They were biding their time, waiting for an opportunity to blow it wide open.

He broached the subject with Agent Black who made a note and did not respond. Roy pressed him, reversing the roles of interviewer and interviewee.

"When you signed up for this job, is this what you thought you'd be doing?"

"It doesn't matter what I think. I serve at the pleasure of the president."

"You're quoting Colin Powell."

Agent Black nodded and let it settle in his gut. He was an older man, mid fifties, clean-shaven, his dark eyes and skin betraying an Indian, Asian or Middle Eastern descent. He reached under the desk and pressed a switch.

"Colin Powell resigned," he said.

Yes, Powell resigned but not before delivering what will be recorded as one of the most deceptive presentations in United Nations history. In laying the groundwork for war with Iraq, replete with charts, photographs and satellite images, the former Secretary of State delivered a package of lies under the label of undeniable fact. Yes, he resigned but not before enabling the little man with an ego the size of Texas to be "reelected" president of the United States.

"A little late, don't you think?" Roy inquired.

"You and I," said Agent Black, "are not as different as one might think. We both love our country. We both believe in freedom and justice. We both want peace."

Roy studied him until he was certain – as certain as circumstances allowed – that he was not being played.

"We're both waiting for a time to act."

Agent Black cocked his head and nodded in a noncommittal gesture. Pointedly, he did not disagree.

The days rolled by and the interviews became shorter and then halted. Agent Black more frequently joined Roy and the others in the community room. They played chess, talked baseball and politics. He found the agent's opinions interesting and informed though they often argued over the role of government. It seemed he was a libertarian and Roy always respected libertarians for their consistency.

Roy noticed that his access to the evening news and political programming was being censored and wondered why. Agent Black fell silent when he inquired.

"You're a prisoner," he said finally. "You haven't forgotten, have you?"

No, he had not. He was mystified at how pleasant his confinement was but he had no illusions. Every minute of every day he resented the sights he could not see, Pike Place Market, the Space Needle, Monks Tavern and the waves rolling down the Straits of Juan de Fuca, the busy sounds of the city, the scent of eucalyptus trees lining their street, the taste of Amy's breath, the intoxication of her touch.

No, he had not forgotten. In some ways he resented their casual politeness. They had lifted him from his life, stolen his purpose for living, denied him the company of friends and loved ones and taken his freedom. Should he be grateful that they made his imprisonment comfortable? If he was an enemy of state, they should treat him as one. If he was not, they should let him go.

"Every night I wake up in the early hours and reach out to the other side of the bed. Every night there is a moment when I'm startled and wonder where she is. Do you know what that's like, Agent Black?"

The agent said nothing. He breathed deeply and retreated to his office.

"No," said Roy to the agent's back, "I haven't forgotten."

A little later Agent Black returned with copies of the *Seattle Times* and the *Washington Post*. He laid them on the table where Roy was sitting.

"It's broken," he said. "It's out in the open."

Roy pick up the *Times* and read the headline top left above the fold:

"Writer Roy Jones Held by Homeland Security."

COUNTERATTACK

Going Public
Waves of Outrage
Finding a Fall Guy

The word went out. It followed a thousand paths to the vast and infinite highways of the worldwide web. Anything that is posted on the web is posted forever – or as long as this technological age endures – indelible and ultimately inalterable.

There was no more holding back. They were in a struggle for survival. One of their own was in detention, no arraignment, no charges, no legal representation and no access to the courts. Miguel Estrada was collateral damage, an unfortunate victim of time and circumstance, but no less abused.

The time for strategic third-party leaks and plants was at an end. Even Sinclair agreed it was time to put all the cards on the table, including the Simon Juneau file. If they wanted a war, they would have one. If they thought the Independent Movement could be crushed with one blow, severing the head of the snake, they were mistaken.

Sara Kent held a press conference in Vancouver to announce a petition for political asylum in behalf of Roman Mason, John Sinclair, Amy Goodall and Freddie

Prader.

This is a story of betrayal at the highest levels of government. This is a case that goes to the heart of American democracy. We will prove beyond doubt that at the behest of both the Republican and Democratic parties, agents of the executive branch – specifically of the Department of Homeland Security – attempted to purge political opposition through acts of terrorism and unlawful detention.

The evidence will show that on the evening of July 20, 2008 said agents launched a concerted attack with firebombs and Molotov cocktails on community activist centers in Seattle, San Francisco, Chicago, Boston and Washington D.C.

The evidence will further show that on the evening of August 1, 2008 said agents conducted an operation with the intent of seizing and detaining the leaders of the Independent Movement, succeeding in the case of Roy Jones. In addition, one Miguel Estrada, an associate of two said leaders, was abducted. Mr. Jones and Mr. Estrada are being held in unknown locations, without charges or representation, as we speak.

What was their crime? Daring to engage in the political process. Daring to build a grassroots political organization dedicated to lawful and peaceful change through the democratic electoral system. Their crime was that they were succeeding.

Representatives of the press, these individuals and the organization they represent, an organization I am proud to be a part of, had absolutely nothing to do with terrorism or global jihad. Plain and simple, this was a political purge.

She introduced her clients and opened the floor to questions. Asked why the government of the United States and the dominant parties would conduct such an operation when their hold on power was absolute and unchallenged, Rome took the microphone.

Arrogance. Unbridled arrogance. They wanted to stop us before we could get a foothold. They wanted to crush us and silence our dissent. But we will not be silent. We are citizens of a nation that is rightly known as the birthplace of democracy – imperfect and profoundly flawed but the principles remain. We were taught from early childhood that if we didn't like how things were it was our right and duty to change it by engaging the process.

They lied to us. They never wanted us to engage the system. In two hundred and forty years of history whenever people have united in a common cause – be it unions or abolitionists or civil rights workers or antiwar activists – those who hold the reigns of power have attempted to crush them. But we struggle on just as they did. They knock us down and we get back up. They spill our blood and we take a vow to remember. They send our sons and daughters to war and we fight back. We resist. We dissent. We are the reason for the Bill of Rights and we will not be cowed.

We know who we are and we know our duty. We are the defenders of liberty and democracy. We are America's last best hope. They can lock us up and throw away the key. They can shoot us down on the streets of protest. Still, we will not be silenced.

Representative Margaret Thomas held another press conference on the steps of Congress calling for hearings on the purge of the Independent Movement.

The call went out for mass protests in every city across the nation, demanding the release of Roy Jones and Miguel Estrada. The American Civil Liberties Union took up the cause, submitting writs of Habeas Corpus. The case was clear for Roy Jones. He was denied his right to due process as a citizen. The case for Miguel Estrada was less so. They would argue that he had entered a contract with the United States government that included his citizenship. He fulfilled the terms of his contract but the government did not, holding him beyond the expiration date on a stop loss order for tour after tour of duty. Moreover, even non-citizens were entitled to some form of due process and judicial review.

The Independent Movement was hardly dead. It was alive and growing, teeming with outrage and spurred by a surge of media reports. Trumpeting a triumph over leftwing domestic terrorists, Hate Radio was on it twenty four seven and contributions were flowing faster than death threats.

A former reporter for the *New York Times* revealed that she had seen a copy of the Juneau file in the Editorial Room. She read enough to know it was a powerful and damning report from a very credible source documenting massive fraud and bipartisan collusion in the last two presidential elections yet *The Times* buried it – unaware that they were not alone in possessing the contents.

At first *The Times* denied the report, labeling its source "a disgruntled employee" but when they were told the reporter had photocopied more than a few pages they reversed course. It was Judy Miller all over again. That reporter famously served as a mouthpiece for the Bush White House with the silent blessings of *The Times* until the Valerie Plame case blew up. Fearful they would be exposed as a fraud once again, they issued a typically convoluted explanation for why they had withheld the story for over three years. They began a series of high-profile reports under the heading: *The Strange Case of Simon Juneau.*

It was all out in the open.

Presidential candidates Barack Obama and John McCain issued statements of outrage and condemnation, denying any personal knowledge or complicity.

Speaker of the House Nancy Pelosi issued a similar statement, commending Representative Thomas and promising a full hearing before the House Judiciary committee.

A *Washington Post* reporter spoke out: "The Democratic Party has been implicated in this story…"

"I can't speak to that," replied the Speaker. "What I can say is: We have a Republican president, a Republican Homeland Security department, and a Republican Party with a history of abuse. The Independent Movement was working with the Obama campaign. Why would they go after an ally?"

The Speaker's eyes grew large as several reporters clamored for a follow up which was not forthcoming. She waved them off with a smile and retreated to her office for a series of consultations with party leaders.

The White House responded in their typical befuddled manner. Having already committed a bushel of impeachable offenses with absolute impunity, one more was inconsequential. A befuddled Dana Perino, the administration's latest experiment in public relations, stated with certainty that Roy Jones and Miguel Estrada would have their day in court. Reminded that both were being held without charges or representation, she began to sweat.

"I'm sure we wouldn't do that without a reason."

Behind closed doors there was widespread panic. Operatives were suddenly unreachable. Members of Congress applied for leave. The Republican and Democratic National Committees were in secret sessions for damage control: Who knew what when and how can we cover it up?

They agreed in concert they needed a fall guy and they were looking to the White House to provide one. Secretary of Homeland Security Michael Chertoff or some appropriate underling seemed a likely candidate for the purge but he could not be blamed for election fraud. That would fall to the recently retired Chief of Staff Karl Rove.

Someone had to pay.

MARCH OF SILENCE

Payback
An Uncertain Future
Tempered Optimism

The word went out, the world took heed and everything that is good and wise said yes, yes, yes. Yes, of course, the government is corrupt beyond redemption. Yes, both parties serve their corporate masters. Yes, we have gone too far, far too far in the war on terror. Yes, we want our rights back. Yes, yes, yes.

The hallowed halls of congress were rife with rumors, accusations and talking points as the House Judiciary Committee prepared for hearings on what was dubbed "Operation Purge." Representative Maggie Thomas of Washington State took her assigned post three chairs to the left of Chairman John Conyers (D-MI).

The first witness called was Homeland Security chief Michael Chertoff. In the manner we have come to expect from officials in the Bush administration, Chertoff consumed forty-five minutes with creative evasion.

The thin man with hollow cheeks, beady eyes and a

shiny bald dome, famed for his inane verbosity, entertained the spectators with tricks of obfuscation. He denied any specific knowledge of the circumstances regarding Roy Jones or Miguel Estrada. His responsibility was confined to administrative oversight; he was not involved in cases on the ground. He admitted only a general knowledge of the Independent Movement and its founder Roman Mason. He could not comment on an investigation in progress.

It was reminiscent of any number of Bush administration testimonies before congress: Attorney General John Ashcroft on domestic surveillance, Attorney General Alberto Gonzalez on the political firing of Justice Department personnel, Secretary of Defense Donald Rumsfeld on war policies, Secretary of State Condoleezza Rice on weapons of mass destruction and Director of Central Intelligence George Tenet on the abuse of intelligence.

Thirty minutes into his testimony, Chertoff wiped the sweat from his brow and resumed an air of indifference. Representative Thomas reminded him that he was aware of the case before the committee and wondered how he could show up so blatantly unprepared.

"With all due respect, Congresswoman, I cannot comment on an investigation in progress."

On and on he droned, deflecting criticism, delivering lectures on the nature of security work, protecting the nation from nefarious actors, serving the nation and honoring the rule of law, without ever really saying anything.

"With all due respect," stated Representative Thomas, "I don't think you or your colleagues in this administration – or indeed in this congress – have paid nearly enough attention to serving the nation and honoring the rule of law."

Again Chertoff wiped his brow, leaned forward to the microphone and said: "I resent the implications and tone of your remarks."

"And I resent that one of my closest friends and colleagues, a man of impeccable honor and integrity, a true American patriot, is locked up in an unknown location under your watch and I have no doubt under your orders."

Chairman Conyers intervened, half apologizing and half empathizing with his colleague for her personal involvement in the case. He did not allow Chertoff to make a clean exit however, expressing disappointment in the quality of his testimony and the forthrightness of his answers. He instructed Chertoff to provide a full account of the information he could not provide in writing within seven days or face contempt charges.

A series of Homeland Security officials followed Chertoff to the witness table, adding little to the proceedings until a middle-aged man of apparent Asian descent calmly entered the halls and swore to tell the truth.

He identified himself as Rhandir Pradesh but his clients and colleagues knew him as Agent Black. He spoke in the low, quiet tone of a proud man who was not proud of the part he had played but was ready to set the record straight.

He testified that he was placed in charge of the assignment they referred to as Operation Purge but was presented by Secretary Chertoff as Operation Squash – a reference to squashing a bug.

"Secretary Chertoff gave you the orders?"

Yes.

"What exactly were those orders?"

We were to take custody of five identified leaders of an organization known as the Independent Movement – Roman Mason, John Sinclair, Amy Goodall, Roy Jones and Fredrick Prader – and an associate – Miguel Estrada – simultaneously within a timeline of seven days. They were to be held in separate facilities under the umbrella of Homeland Security. I was told that the five organization leaders would not resist but that Mr. Estrada, an army private absent without leave, might be armed. We were to take every precaution that Mr. Estrada was not killed. It was my understanding that they intended to "turn" Mr. Estrada to incriminate the others by offering amnesty and full citizenship.

"Did Mr. Chertoff explain why these individuals were being detained?"

He identified the organization as a terrorist group, implicated in the bombing of their own facilities a week prior to the order.

"Did you agree with Mr. Chertoff's assessment?"

After examining the facts of the case, I did not agree.

"Did you communicate your misgivings to the Secretary?"

I said nothing. A man in my position does not question his superior. But he understood.

"How do you know he understood?"

There are ways to communicate one's feelings without words.

Everyone in the crowded hearing room understood by the expression on the agent's face. There was no pleasure in his giving testimony. There were only grave misgivings. He paused to clear his throat and take a sip of water.

"How did Mr. Chertoff respond to your misgivings?"

He said the orders came from the president and he expected them to be carried out with due diligence.

"You were ordered to detain six individuals but you only detained two. Can you explain your apparent incompetence?"

When agents do not believe in the case, it frequently happens that there are lapses in the execution of their duties.

Agent Pradesh, with the even-tempered patience of a trained professional, survived a series of attempts to impugn his character, including one congressman's questions regarding his ethnic background, and left the chambers with his head held high.

Within a week Secretary Chertoff joined the legions of high-level officials to resign from the administration of George W. Bush: Colin Powell, George Tenet, Donald Rumsfeld, John Ashcroft, Alberto Gonzalez, Richard Perle, Paul Wolfowitz, Richard Clarke, Paul O'Neill, Lewis "Scooter" Libby, Karl Rove, Eric Shinseki, Anthony Zinni, Michael Brown, Larry Linsey, Ann Wright, John Kiesling, Scott McClellan, John Brown, Rand Beers, Karen Kwiatkowski, Charles Pritchard, Paul Redmond, Joanne Wilson, Martha Hahn, Rich Biondi, Alphonso Jackson on and on and on. Some were pushed out for not honoring the loyalty code; others were caught committing high crimes and misdemeanors, while still others could no longer recognize themselves in the mirror.

The only recognizable figures left in the inner circle of the Bush White House were Josh Bolten, Andrew Card and Condoleezza Rice. It was a tragic story of an infectious disease or a malignant cancer that consumed everything and everyone within its reach.

It would almost be worthy of tears if not for the knowledge that the administration's demise set good men and women free.

Roy Jones and Miguel Estrada were released. Estrada was granted a pardon, an honorable discharge and full rights of citizenship in exchange for his silence on the "harsh interrogation" techniques used in his confinement. He could have pressed it but he wanted his freedom far more than he wanted revenge.

Even before its findings were published, the House Judiciary Committee issued an apology to Roy, Miguel and everyone associated with the Independent Movement. Amy, Rome and Sinclair returned to Seattle under their own names and were not accosted by any agent of the United States government.

Amy and Roy happily reunited. The organization they served to provide refuge to dissidents was severely compromised so they founded a new organization, above board with the same objectives through fundraising, lobbying, legal representation and public relations.

On the heels of the Juneau report Karl Rove was finally indicted for his part in the Valerie Plame affair, illegal wiretapping, election fraud and giving false testimony to congress. Other operatives of both parties were spared criminal indictment but the stain on their reputations was imprinted in the public record.

Lacking time and courage to initiate the impeachment process, both houses of congress managed to pass a blanket censure of the White House during the Bush years for demeaning the constitution and dishonoring the nation.

Candidates Obama and McCain issued condemnations, apologies and the standard disclaimer: If anyone involved in my campaign had anything to do with this case, not only will they be fired but prosecuted to the full extent of the law. The frightening thing was that both men seemed to believe they possessed that kind of authority.

Back in Seattle, the Independent Movement issued a call for a March of Silence in Washington D.C. not only to acknowledge the release of their colleagues but also to pave the way for the future of the movement.

Once the bombs began falling on Baghdad, our government all but demanded that we honor a code of silence. We were not silent then and we will not be silent now. And yet, in a world where the language of irony is lost like an ancient tongue never committed to tablet, perhaps the best answer lies in a language they are not familiar with: A March of Silence.

Let us gather together in tens and thousands, to drape ourselves in solemn black, to march in deafening silence, to dissent in silence, to mourn in silence, to cry out in silence for those who can longer cry out and to honor the silence of oppression and death.

So the activists of the Independent Movement put out the word and the people responded. They came by the tens and hundreds, they reported by the thousands, ready and willing to play their part.

In late September, two months before the presidential election, a mass of citizens draped in black converged on Lafayette Park in Washington. They lined up, shoulder to shoulder, line after line, and marched step by step in funereal procession down 17th Street, past the White House to Constitution Avenue and on to Lincoln Memorial on the National Mall.

On the steps of the Memorial where once Martin Luther King Jr. stood, speakers addressed a growing mass of solemn, silent protestors. They decried the inherent corruption of the two-party system and the folly of perpetual pragmatism: the lesser of two evils.

Rome was the last to speak.

We are not here to celebrate a victory. We have not ended the war in Iraq. We are no closer to ending the occupation of Afghanistan. Blood is being spilled in our names even as we gather here today.

We have not ended the reign of corporate government or the corruption that dominates our political process. We have not restored the Bill of Rights, the principle of Habeas Corpus or confidence in our democracy.

But we have made a start. We are cautiously optimistic. We only ask that you do not depart from this gathering, this place of historic wonder, this monument to freedom, this symbol of justice and democracy, thinking that we have accomplished something great.

We ask that you do not forget the crimes of authority, the abuse of power that brought us together on this occasion. It is important to look back in anger at what became of our nation when we were too busy or too hungry to pay attention and engage. It is as important to look back in anger, as it is to look forward in hope.

A great man, a citizen of the world and one of our most heroic founders, once said: We have it in our power to begin the world over again. We have it in our hands to make the world anew.

What happened today is monumental. But what happens tomorrow and tomorrow and tomorrow, after we return to our homes and cities across the nation, will determine whether this great experiment of American democracy will endure.

PART II

THE CORPORATE OVERLORDS

APRIL 2012

HIDDEN TRUTHS & REVELATIONS

Big Brother Strikes Back
Nip it in the Bud
The Overlords

If you think you've won, that you're now in the clear, that you've defeated the monster with the world watching, that you've exposed our corrupt government for all to see, and therefore you cannot be touched, you have much to learn. The government is only a small player in the arena you've entered and you are the gladiators. This is not a Hollywood film. In the real world, gladiators always lose. Gladiators enter with glory and exit to the grave.

You may think I am your enemy but I am only the messenger. You may think I wish you harm but I wish to spare you harm. They will come for your family. They will come for your friends. They will come for their families. They will come for your loved ones. Then they will come for you. You may think I am one of them but I am...

Your friend.

Rome received the encrypted message through a web site designed for maximum privacy and protected by multiple layers of security code. Whoever sent it wanted him to know he possessed the knowledge and technology of an insider.

He circulated the message to his core group and then posted it on the web with a challenge to the activist hacker community to uncover the identity of the sender. If anyone could do it, he felt certain they could. If they could not, then the enemy was as formidable as it seemed and more so.

He could do nothing but wait and think. Hamlet's disease, he could think in ever expanding circles. He could spin webs that would make Queen Mab pale with envy. He could think until his brain pulsated and his body suffered from lack of sleep. Knowing his disease, he knew where it led and determined not to go there.

Still, the constant calculation of risk-reward had to be made. He had long ago concluded that there were powers in the world far greater than the government. Hardly a conspiracy theory, compelling evidence presented itself in his daily consumption of news. No one with eyes to see and an open mind could fail to absorb it.

Governments large and small did the bidding of their controllers. Corporations large and small fronted for them. Dictators and tyrants bowed to them. Knowledgeable societies, the Masons, the Rosicrucians and the Illuminati, spoke and wrote of them but none could identify their members or their methodology. Known as the secret societies, they could never pierce the shield of the true elite, the controllers, the puppet masters or the overlords as the case may be.

The only way to hide, then as now, is in plain sight.

He could not stop his mind from chasing down the possibilities. He had not contemplated the question of the overlords in many years. When he had, he hypothesized that the organizational structure was familial. As an organization they left no mark. They had no legacy. People of power do not wish to remain anonymous. The hypothesis led to the speculation that the organization consisted at its pinnacle of the most famous and wealthy families in history: The Rothschilds, the Du Ponts, the Rockefellers, the Vanderbilts, the Morgan family, the Carnegies and the Melons, on and on. The families represented old wealth, aristocratic wealth, and the power followed the bloodline through generations. The inevitable power struggles would be shielded from public scrutiny by the nature of the family. Family matters remain private.

It all came back like an awakening, like a thunderclap, like a flood of memories, like a revelation. The truth. The truth. It had been so long since he could even conceive of anything called the truth. The truth is not a conundrum. It is not an insoluble equation. It is not an unknowable abstraction beyond the reach of mortal man. The truth is the truth. It springs from an eternal void and strikes you down with the force of a sledgehammer. The truth is an undeniable reality. The truth is that which remains when all else abandons. The truth is a hole, a cage, an obscure island from which there is no escape.

He saw the truth though no one in his circle from his closest friends to his bitter enemies would recognize it. The truth. Why had it taken him until now when he could do nothing to change it? The overlords reached back through recorded time, as old as history itself. No one had been able to reveal them, no less to stop them. Why now?

Times change.

The most game changing development in all of history occurred when the internet came online. No longer would humans write history to their own ends. The web recorded all human affairs. The web existed as living history. Moreover, the web created a separate and enduring reality. Those who could control the web would control the legacy of all who resided on the planet. The web could not be turned off even if we wanted to do so. It exists above and beyond our mortal lives, much like the overlords themselves.

The question remained: Why would an organization as powerful and omnipotent as the overlords concern themselves with the machinations of his little group and his modest political movement? They had won a dozen congressional races and converted a half dozen more. They had a place in modern political history. Never had a third party or independent movement had such success but they hardly threatened the established order. Why would the overlords target them?

Nip it in the bud. The word goes out on the web and spreads. Success breeds success. What begins as a wave becomes a tsunami and the world changes. Fundamental change. Is that not what he wanted, what he worked for, and what he dreamed of his entire adult life?

He made a modest meal, sipped a fine red wine, a cabernet from Mendocino, answered a few calls and listened to Thelonious Monk. It soothed him. He would meet with the core the following evening. Tonight he would relax. He knew what he must do. To reveal the truth, he needed the assistance of the most brilliant technological minds on the earth. He had to make contact with the group known as Anonymous.

A loose confederation of rebel hackers, if anyone could do the job they could.

He slept well that night and dreamed of the overlords. He joined them in a private, luxury suite overlooking the proceedings at the Bilderberg conference. Down below on the conference floor, presidents, prime ministers, senators, parliamentary leaders, chief executive officers, military commanders and intelligence officials, all the men and women perceived as the power brokers of the world, discussed the business of the day. Every now again an overlord would pick up a phone and ring one of the officials on the floor. All eyes turned and all ears listened to what the official said next.

It could not be clearer who held the true reigns of power.

SHOT OFF THE BOW

Maneuverings
Bolstering Defenses
Decoys and Deceptions

They took every precaution they could think to take. They added layers of security both at home and the office. Freddie Prader studied code for twenty-four hours, trying to track the message to its source. He collapsed in exhaustion. He thought he might have a lead or two but could not be certain. Whoever or whatever entity lay behind the intrusion, they possessed the highest level of technological wizardry. Even if he managed to find the right path, a hacker of this caliber would just reroute and cover, a minor inconvenience. He felt the best course of action would be to redesign his security system from the bottom up with decoys and traps. With a little luck, he might lure the hacker into revealing himself.

No one in the core group thought it a hoax. They had crossed a border, violated the code of conduct, and in so doing they had exceeded the threshold of influence. The powers they fought against, the major parties, the established order, the corporate oligarchs, would not sit still for this trespass. They would fight back.

They had embarrassed the government. Then they had taken seats in the sacred halls of congress, seats reserved for members only. It surprised them that they would announce their intentions. They deduced that the message came from an ally, known or unknown, inside their organization or (more likely) inside their adversary's organization. He wanted to warn them and the question was: Why?

They decided against wasting their resources chasing down the intruder. Let him make contact but make sure he or she or they cannot gain access to private information. Make sure the Messenger (as they entitled him) could do no harm.

Freddie scratched his head just below his left ear and shriveled his nose, raising the level of his wire-rimmed glasses: Easy to say. Not easy to do. He sought to clarify their instructions: You want me to let him through for a message but block him from everything else? Nods around the table circled back to his silence. He didn't know that it could be done but agreed to try. They hoped that the Messenger would be true to his signature: friend, not foe. Rome wanted to recruit him. To accomplish that they had to allow contact; they had to invite him in even if it meant exposing them to harm. Risk and reward.

They next discussed setting up a new headquarters and relocating to Vancouver, reasoning that if the NSA or the American intelligence community targeted them, it would be more difficult to accomplish across the border – at least legally. Roy and Amy could move at a moment's notice. Sara and Freddie would take a week or two. Rome would maintain his residencies in Seattle and on the Sound while seeking dual citizenship. Sinclair decided against the move though he agreed it might add a measure of protection. *I'm too old to start up in a new house, a new community.* He had no family and the only friends he had sat around this table preparing to move away. *I've been dying for a decade,* he reasoned. *If they kill me I'll become a martyr to the cause.* What better death could he wish for? He would remain in Seattle.

"I'll write my obituary," he said with a wry grin.

As a member of congress, Maggie would have to remain behind. Miguel Estrada had a political career in Colorado. Everyone else would pick up and move. Amy and Roy would employ their organization to secure housing with a maximum degree of anonymity. Like Rome, they would seek dual citizenship. Canada had ultimately been good to them and Sara, familiar with Canadian law, would expedite the process.

Sinclair gave a positive report on the political front. Their network of community activist centers continued to grow in the aftermath of the march in Washington. Each center had a political branch that provided a constant update on the prospects for success in local and congressional elections. Each center recruited and cultivated possible candidates and reported every week to the national organization. Now it seemed they would have to be more careful about communications. If Freddie could not guarantee security, they would have to consider old-school means of communication.

The old man sat on his porch, rocking and reading from a tattered book of poetry: Love Poems by Pablo Neruda. A very special gift from an old friend he had not seen in a long, long time, he had read it enough that he could feel the indentures of his fingers on the leather binding. He glanced up from time to time to gaze at the open fields, the distant mountains, and to keep an eye on his niece as she learned to ride her first bicycle.

She struggled to stay afloat like a child learning to swim, arms and elbows flailing. The first lesson is balance. He taught her to gain her balance, to feel gravity and find her center, and then he let her go. You can only teach a child so much. The rest is trial and error. She had already experienced her first fall. She knew instinctively how to angle her body for a soft landing. Now she had the hang of it. Her dark brown eyes glowed with knowing and the thrill of flying, the wind lifting her dark hair. He beheld her beauty, beauty in motion. Innocence, charm, grace and wonder. Pure joy.

She became a part of him. She claimed a place in his heart. She had lost her father, a common affliction in the community it seemed, and her mother found friends and family members to look after her while her mother worked. Little Juliet could have stayed with any number caretakers. She brightened the lives of anyone she accompanied. But she chose to stay with Papa, the old man, El Viejo Marcos and his wife Margarit. In some ways she reminded him of a young boy he knew and nurtured years ago. He thought of him now and as he gazed at the chair where that boy once sat, reading aloud the book he now held, a speeding car appeared as if out of nowhere.

In a fraction of a second he recognized the danger and time slowed as if to amplify an unfolding tragedy. A large sedan, a dark blue Pontiac, barreled down the road toward a little girl balancing her bike. He could see the driver's eyes grow larger as the old man stood to yell. Before he could do either, the driver hit his brakes, screaming and skidding as little Juliet tumbled and fell. He sprinted to the roadside as fast as his old legs could pump, his wife and a neighbor down the road following. He lifted her with the strength of a young man and carried her to the house even as the neighbor yelled not to move her.

She cried and screamed but only fear had harmed her. The old man willed that car to stop and in a slow-motion miracle it did no more than a yard from impact. He did not wait to talk to the driver; he sat in his swing on the porch and rocked her until her cries surrendered and the last tear she wiped away.

The driver, a Mexican man unknown to him, walked to the porch and apologized in a voice and manner that seemed in retrospect far too calm. El Viejo did not wish to engage him and neither did his wife so he walked back to his car and drove away. They did not watch him go. They did not study his face, his build or notice his license plate or any other details of his clothing or vehicle. Their only concern was that their little girl was safe.

Would it have made a difference had they paid more attention? They would never know. They knew only that their beautiful little girl had escaped a terrible fate.

They had chocolate ice cream and allowed Juliet to watch television shows and play inside until her mother came for her. They told her what had happened in as much detail as they dared, exchanged hugs of relief, and her mother took Juliet home.

After supper, a man knocked on their door and asked to speak to El Viejo. The old man looked in his eyes and knew it was about Juliet and the racing car that nearly ended her young life. He had seen this man but did not know him. He gave a name (whether it was his real name he did not know and would not wish to know) and said he had been paid to deliver a message. He had sad eyes that said he did not enjoy the task but he had no choice. The message was this: The incident with the little girl was not an accident. It was a warning. He told the old man that he must deliver a message to his friend Miguel. He said the people that paid him and carried out the warning would know if he failed to deliver the message. He would tell Miguel about what had happened with the words: This was a shot off the bow. Miguel would deliver the same message to his friend Roman.

Blood rushed to the old man's face and his hands trembled. The man gave him a phone number and left with a quiet apology. El Viejo would carry the message forward. He understood. He had no choice.

HEAD OF A SNAKE

Information and Power
Cease and Desist
Check and Mate

Some play poker, some play the market, some play golf and some like Roman Mason and William Sinclair play chess. No matter the game, there comes a time when the player recognizes the end game. You throw in your cards, you sell your shares, you shake your opponent's hand or turn over your king. You take your losses and go home.

Rome received the message loud and clear. He texted the circle: *All plans on hold. Emergency meeting, usual place and time.*

Miguel Estrada jumped on a plane to Seattle. Maggie remained in Washington. Rome would inform her later of their actions. Everyone else gathered together in the back room of the Monastery, its thick gray walls adding to the sullen mood of the circle.

Miguel informed them what had happened, his eyes filled with tears as he described his relationship with El Viejo and the love the old man had for the little girl who came so close to death. "If not for El Viejo, I don't know what would have happened to me but I know I wouldn't be here today."

They went around the circle, trying to find answers and solutions to a problem that clearly threatened their existence. Who are they? What is their motivation? Rome offered his theory, his speculation really, that they were above the government and beyond what we typically think of as the corporate elite. He did not go into detail. He did not feel it necessary. He had engaged most of them in late night discussions of the Carlyle Group and the Brandenburg conference, though he did not proffer his ideas concerning the elite families and hereditary succession.

How did their political enterprise threaten the all-powerful elite? It did not. It only interfered with their agenda. Even in small numbers, their representatives in congress and state legislatures managed to push back anti-labor laws, privatization of education laws and immunity for corporate polluters. They tipped the balance and shamed enough Democrats into standing up for their constituents to make a difference.

They can't allow our numbers to grow. Success spawns success and our ideas, our ideals, spread across the political spectrum.

Why didn't they go after the candidates rather than the central organization? They did. They had. But they suffered a credibility problem. Information is power and the Independent Movement possessed information. They could go after an opposing candidate with greater effect. Too often they won in the contest of political attack and counterattack.

They perceive us as a small but dangerous snake. How do you kill a snake? You cut off its head.

Why did they take this specific action? Why did they choose to target a child, an innocent, while under the care of an old man? The child not related to the old man, the old man not related to Miguel, and yet the bonds of affection were as strong as any family.

They want us to know that their knowledge, their information network, reaches far beyond anything we have yet encountered. They want us to know that we can't protect our people. It's impossible. They want us to know that no one, not even a child, is safe.

They discussed the possibilities, tracking them down, going to the press, negotiating a compromise, but it all led back to the stone cold fact that they could not protect their people. Rome had already gone round and round. He had already arrived at the conclusion they now fought against reaching.

We're done as an organization. We don't know who they are and we can't take the risks. We don't know how far they'll go but we can be sure they won't stop until they've accomplished their goal, until they've dismantled us or rendered us irrelevant.

Stunned by Rome's proclamation, they stared at him and at each other in disbelief. They had all worked hard and risked everything for the cause but no one had lost a life or a loved one. The government played by a set of rules that rarely allowed the murder of innocent civilians (beyond war or military actions). This unknown enemy crossed all borders of decency. They played like the mob or the cartels. Were they willing to cross that line themselves? No. Their weakness was their decency. Would they risk the lives of innocents? No, they would not. Not knowingly. Not with the certainty that this enemy appeared to present.

The night would be long and filled with drink. They came to a meeting that became a wake for their movement. Miguel shook Rome's hand, thanked him, and thanked them all for what had done not only for him but also for his old friend and the child he did not yet know. Spent and anxious to get back to Colorado, he excused himself and departed, hoping that fate would someday bring them together again under more pleasant circumstances.

Rome took his usual place in the corner of the public room where a young jazz quartet played a set inspired by the experimental jazz greats: Coltrane, Monk, the Bird, Miles, Mingus and the immortal Ornette Coleman. He ordered a pitcher of ale and held court. One by one and two by two, members of the core circle joined him to share their private thoughts. Early to rise, early to leave Freddie first approached him, taking the seat to his right. He said he understood the decision but he felt like he lost his family.

Does that make me a father figure?

More like an uncle.

He wanted to know if Rome still had an interest in the Messenger. Rome nodded and grabbed his arm when Freddie went for his wallet. He poured a glass of ale and whispered: Wait until you're leaving and put it on the table with your tip. Freddie sipped his ale and listened to the band until they finished their set. He pulled out a dollar and left it on the table along with a business card with instructions scrawled on the back for contacting the Messenger. Back to the stage, he whispered: *This guy is serious and he wishes to remain Anonymous.* Rome pulled out a couple dollars to supplement the tip and palmed the card into his coat pocket as Freddie slipped out the door into a grim Seattle night.

Amy and Roy joined him with another pitcher of ale. They too understood and respected the decision but they did not agree. A child's life had been threatened but no one died. Where would civil rights be if the movement stopped with the first bashed head or the first burning cross? Where would the unions be if they backed down with the first hammer blow of the Pinkerton pigs? Where would the antiwar movement have gone if they weren't willing to sacrifice?

Where are they now?

He didn't mean to be cynical though he had fought through the fog of cynicism most of his life. He knew and embraced the importance of protest and civil disobedience. The antiwar movement shaped his character and crystallized his perception of the world. But now he watched elections turn on the disenfranchisement of tens of thousands of minority voters, the loss of privacy and privacy protections, the gradual disappearance of unions from the workforce and he wondered, he had to wonder, if all the struggle, blood and tears, had been in vain. He did not believe that. He could not believe it. But doubt invaded his soul in dark moments like fruit flies in an overripe peach.

I know. If we don't continue the struggle, we'll lose what we've gained. I don't expect you stop fighting. You can be sure I won't stop fighting. We'll just fight in a different way. Do what you can. Do what you must. And stay in touch. I would only ask that you be discreet.

Neither Amy nor Roy pressed him. They understood the need to circumnavigate a sensitive subject even with friends. They knew the need for discretion in their own organization. Need to know was more than a cliché; it was a way of life. They shook hands and embraced not knowing when, where or how they would meet again but feeling certain that they would. They had their own cause, their own organization, and they would continue the work. But they also cared deeply for the Independent Movement and they would find a way to help. They would not stand by while the most important political development in modern history died. They hoped and believed Rome felt the same.

Sara Kent had worked professionally with Rome longer than anyone, longer than Sinclair and longer than Maggie. With the exception of Maggie, she knew him better than anyone. She knew that the decision to dissolve the core group did not mean capitulation. She and Sinclair both knew it represented a change of strategy. To what end they did not know. They joined him now to see what they could learn.

I saw you two over there. Conspiring I presume. I wondered how long it would take you to visit me.

We had to wait our turn.

The band played their third set, a particularly experimental piece, scattered and wild, a completely original work, improvisational with a theme that spoke to the moment: death and rebirth, transformation, evolution. They created violent chaos, fought back and tamed the beast only to unleash a greater evil. The battle raged on.

I like this band. They speak to me.

I prefer Mozart.

Me? The Rolling Stones.

There's a place for all of us. That is the miracle of life on earth.

They listened for a spell, putting their thoughts in storage, letting go in order to enjoy the moment. When jazz is right it flies like an eagle, like a missile, like a bullet at the moon, and then it dives, submerged in the depths, it slows and crawls until it finds the surface and soars again. Blues is the music of the heart. Jazz is the mind, the maze of cognitive pathways, the soul of the creative impulse, a map of the human brain. As a chess player, Sinclair admired the attraction though he preferred the relative order of classical. Sara, rock to the heart, felt the rhythm and the pulse of Rome's divergent mind, never to be underestimated, never to be contained, never predictable. As the piece drew to its final notes, Rome sighed in appreciation, certain that the band had captured and held its audience in abandon, satisfied and at peace.

Have you come to a conclusion?

They had but they did not expect to be tested. If they were on point, Rome would inform them of his designs in due time. Sara lacked the patience for mind games that both men found engaging. Her gift for drawing a conclusion pushed her forward.

You and Sinclair have no family, no friends to speak of except those involved in the Independent Movement. You're cutting the movement loose, hoping that it survives on its own merit, in order to protect its members and loved ones. You will engage this new enemy whom we will call the Overlords. You will need a lawyer but one who is not directly involved. That's where I come in. How am I doing?

Rome smiled. Always impressed by the acuity of her reasoning, he wondered if his new enemy would as easily see through his deception. He had Maggie and her family to consider. He hoped that her lack of involvement and her status as a member of congress would add a layer of protection but he could not be sure. He would walk a tightrope and hope that the enemy would not be so quick to decipher the code as Sara had. He needed time to uncover the Overlord hierarchy so that any further actions like the threat aimed at a little girl would come at a price.

I will be establishing a residency in Vancouver after all. I would like to retain your services to expedite my application for dual citizenship. In the course of this expedition, I have reason to believe I will need further services in the areas of privacy rights, the rights of whistleblowers, civil disobedience and international asylum. I will need someone well versed in internet law, Canadian law, American and international law.

Sara rose, shook hands and kissed him on the cheek. Nothing more needed to be said or explained. Nothing more could be said without exposing her to danger. Nothing more except: *Be careful.* They watched her go with admiring eyes before Sinclair raised his glass of ale.

Well, old friend, once again it's you and I against the world.

MEDIUM AND MESSAGE

Opening Moves
Players and Pretenders
Bait and Trap

Late the following day, after he had cleared his brain of the night's overindulgence, after he had talked to Maggie and persuaded her that he was not on the verge of breakdown, he put out a message to every chapter of the Independent Movement:

Dear Member
It has been my pleasure to be at the forefront of the Independent Movement these past seven years. During this time I have gotten to know most of you as extraordinary and talented community leaders. Together we have made history. We have launched an effective challenge to the major party stranglehold on American electoral politics. I am and will always be proud of our achievements. With the certainty that the cause and the movement will live on and thrive in your capable hands, the time has come for me and my associates in the core leadership group to step aside and allow the grassroots to take control.
We ask that you seize this opportunity and move forward as we continue to support the cause, each in his and her

individual way.

The Messenger made contact and wanted a meeting at a secure location to be determined. Rome called from a rare pay phone at a downtown cafe. The communication was cryptic and brief. He would send instructions by courier. With irony worthy of a political commentator, the Messenger did not trust the medium.

Bicycle in tow, the courier appeared at his door with a small package. Nothing in his expression betrayed anything out of the ordinary. He tipped him and watched him scurry down the hallway to the elevator. The package contained a simple note: Bainbridge Ferry, 12:20 tomorrow. Portside bow.

Grateful that he did not have to dash out on a cold damp night, he met Sinclair for dinner at Anthony's overlooking the Sound. They discussed the possibilities, precautions that should be taken and strategies for their campaign against the Overlords over seafood and a fine bottle of Zinfandel. Sinclair held the opinion that the Messenger could not be trusted until tested.

Wearing a wool sweater, a heavy hooded jacket over his arm, Rome boarded the ferry thirty minutes before departure. He climbed to the deck where boarders claimed seats on both sides of the vessel. Looking over his shoulder, he bought a large coffee and strolled to the portside bow. He waited for the ferry to embark before putting his coat on, zipping up and walking outside to greet the chill of the Sound. Concerned at how easy it would be for a couple of thugs to toss a man overboard, he sat tight to the wall and kept his hand on the stun gun he carried in his coat pocket.

Before long a thin young man in dark glasses and three layers of clothing, the hood of his sweatshirt pulled over his head, emerged from the warmth inside and sat beside him.

Mr. Mason.

Who are you?

I am Anonymous. I'm sorry about the cold but we had to be sure (a) that no one was following you and (b) that they couldn't monitor our conversation.

They? Who are they?

That's the question.

He smiled and it revealed his youth. Young people are often brilliant beyond their experience but they tend to be overconfident and they enjoy their own wit a little too much. Anonymous seemed to catch Rome's skepticism and his smile dissolved like a sugar cube in hot tea.

Still live with your parents?

That's an overused cliché.

Do you?

No. Smile. *I moved out six months ago.* Smile. *Three months.*

Rome liked this kid. He reminded him of Freddie, barely able to grow a decent beard but blessed with a keen mind and a sharp sense of humor. Like Freddie, he probably excelled in high school academics, failed with girls, graduated early to escape a world that jocks rule and earned a degree in less than two years. He made his friends on the web and found his people. Now he lived in their world, on the side of righteousness but too often on the other side of the law.

We've got people on the inside. They recruit us, you know. The thing is: The ones they recruit were caught. The ones on the outside were not.

You're better than they are.

They have the money. They buy the best technology. But we have the brains.

What do you want from me?

They tested you. You capitulated too easy. They either think you're lying or they own you. You're smart and rich. They want you to work for them.

He gazed out at the Sound, the power of the sea moving the ferry from side to side, the beauty and the force that always inspired his greater ambitions. Everything the kid said made sense. But could he be trusted?

We want you to join them but work for us.

How do I know you weren't recruited? How do I know you don't work for them?

I've been thinking about that and I have no answers. I don't know what we could do to prove our allegiance. I can tell you what I know: I know they're monitoring your communications – phone, email, everything electronic.

Who is? The NSA?

The kid looked at him as if to say: You're not as smart as we thought you were, as if his brain lacked a quadrant, as if his perception fell one dimension short.

Who gathers data for the NSA?

Booz Allen Hamilton, the Carlyle Group. They're using government data for their own purposes?

Does that surprise you?

It's illegal.

Nobody cares.

Nobody cares if nobody knows.

We'd like to change that.

Who's behind it?

We don't know. The Carlyle Group? The Rothschilds?

The Rockefellers? The bankers? The International Monetary Fund? The World Bank? Maybe the myth is reality. They take both sides in every conflict. They guide Israel into existence and finance the Nazis. They kill presidents and plot terrorist events. Nobody knows. That's what we intend to find out. That's why we need you. A man of your stature and intellect. You're just the kind of man they would allow entry into their sanctum. We intend to uncover them, document what they've done and what they're doing and what they envision for all of us. When we do we'll post it on the web. In the words of George Herbert Walker Bush: a thousand points of light. They'll deny it of course but we'd have you to back us up. An eyewitness of unimpeachable integrity, a firsthand account from the heart of the beast. You exposed the government; now you could expose the corporate overlords. That's the dream.

Can you protect my people?

Rome asked knowing that they could not. Maybe he meant it as a test. Would they lie to further their interests? If they did, what would it mean?

We think you've taken the best available measure short term. Over the long run you need leverage: some incriminating piece of evidence, something powerful enough to hold them in check.

As they approached the end of the crossing, both realized they had only opened a line of communication. They would not reach an agreement today. They would leave this meeting with an open mind. Rome needed more information and a stronger foundation for trust. The young man who identified himself as Anonymous understood.

With your permission, we'll contact you by the same means. If you need to contact us for immediate assistance, call this number and hang up. We'll know.

He handed Rome a card as he shook hands, careful that any monitors in the vicinity could not pick it up.

I don't need to tell you: You should stay for lunch. An immediate return would attract attention.

You think they're watching us?

No. But we have to assume they are.

He went his way, leaving Rome to contemplate a plethora of possibilities. Beyond question the kid had achieved his goal: He was impressed.

NEW BEGINNINGS

Compensating for Loss
Taking Chances
Paying the Price

Amy and Roy wasted no time, pressing on with their dual cause of aiding dissidents and building a political movement. Amy took on the task of researching candidates and prospective candidates in promising districts. Roy expanded his duties from shaping the message of the movement to fundraising. Not content to allow their electoral gains to stagnate or regress, they doubled their efforts and actively recruited new talent.

Working alongside them late into the night, running numbers and doing analyses, Freddie encountered an anomaly and traced it to a source that caught his attention. It did not surprise him that Booz Allen Hamilton had hacked into their system. A technology and security corporation, specializing in information and surveillance, the company had a distinct interest in political outcomes and their tentacles extended in all directions. It did surprise him that he could trace the hack back to their expansive NSA data-gathering compound as well as the office of the Vice President and former Director of National Intelligence under

George W. Bush, Mike McConnell. Tapping NSA data or using NSA resources to attack a political campaign or for any other non-government business had to be illegal. Instinctively, he hacked the system to see if he could gather incriminating evidence.

In a matter of seconds he realized he had made a critical mistake. The security monitors revealed a flurry of activity outside the building. Seven men emerged from a van parked on the street below, one in a grey suit and six in FBI jackets, rifles in hand. Four of the six armed men dashed for the front entrance to the building while the other two went to cover the rear exit. The man in the suit followed them through the front exit, sounding an alarm that quickly silenced.

What's going on?

Prone to paralysis at times of crisis, Freddie struggled to find words but the only utterance to emerge from his mouth was: *FBI.* The agents were storming up the stairs. They would crash through the door in less than three minutes.

Is there any way out?

The tech center had been raided before. They had a contingency plan but neither Amy nor Roy knew about it. The old building had a service elevator that had not been functional in a decade. They refurbished it just for this occasion. He had altered the electronic blueprints so that an invader would not know about it unless they consulted the original hard copy in city hall. Who did that these days?

Follow me!

He hustled to the elevator located behind a wall of servers so that it could not be seen from the working center. He ushered them inside, pushed the down button, handed Amy his cell phone, closed the grate and as the elevator crept quietly but slowly downward, he instructed them to wait for his signal before making their escape. They wanted to ask questions but they sensed the intense immediacy of his actions. Freddie covered the elevator with a long cardboard box designed for the purpose. Then he rushed to push a heavy desk to the door and resumed his position at the control center, watching the agents close in, hearing them announce FBI! and pounding in the door.

He stood and held up his hands, watching them go through their FBI routine, making sure no perpetrators lurked behind a desk or in a hall closet. One by one the agents called out Clear! and formed a circle around him, their weapons pointed at his chest.

Hands on your head, now!

Freddie complied as one of the agents patted him down and instructed him to sit. He did. The monitors distributed around the center recorded the events and transferred the images to Freddie's cell phone where Amy and Roy could observe. The man in the suit walked in and looked around before lowering his eyes to meet Freddie's.

Is he the only one here?

Yes, sir.

You're sure.

Yes, sir.

You think you're pretty clever, don't you?

Yes, sir.

The suit studied him like a man reading the back cover to reveal the content of a book to see if it was worth reading.

May I lower my hands?

Yes, you may.

He did so in an awkward manner, with a wave of his hand, and the suit noticed. The book suddenly got more interesting.

What was that?

What was what?

He looked around with keener interest, walked behind the servers and tossed the cardboard box aside.

Clever boy. No one noticed the elevator?

They looked at each other like children caught in an act of vandalism. How could they know? They'd studied the blueprints.

The suit signaled the agents on the street and said: We've got perps on the run. Secure the building. Meantime, Amy and Roy walked outside, hugged the wall until they made it to their car and drove at speed limit several blocks before turning off the main road. Once again, they were outlaws on the run with nowhere to go.

THE HACKER'S CODE

Blowback
Friends in High Places
Free Freddie!

Freddie Prader had family, parents, grandparents, aunts, uncles, nieces, nephews and in-laws, who would notice within days that Freddie had disappeared without a trace. He also had friends in the hacker community who would know with minutes what had happened.

He designed a system that would instantly alert the hacker community in the event of an emergency. The instant the FBI began meddling with his files, the code along with the recorded images of what took place went out to every hacker in the community.

There is a code by which the hacker lives and one of the cardinal principles is: You have a right to hack back. If someone, anyone, whether a government agency, a private corporation or another hacker, invades your space, you have a right and a duty to invade theirs. Within minutes of reviewing the recorded event and the computer code, without regard for law or authority, the community knew he had done no wrong. He had only acted by the code. It became their collective duty to exonerate him or barring that to exact a price.

Within twenty-four hours a website went up under the title: Free Freddie! It contained a chronicle of the event, a downloadable recording and source code. When the authorities attacked, for every site that went down two emerged with an additional account of the latest attack and its source code. The site's popularity grew exponentially. Within days the site went around the world and back again, the activist community had a new hero, and the family emerged to speak out in behalf of Freddie. His parents took interviews first with Democracy Now, then MSNBC and CNN. At every gathering of activists, the cry went out: Free Freddie! Free Freddie! Free Freddie!

The FBI released a statement: *Frederick Paul Prader is being held by Homeland Security on suspicion of espionage. It is alleged that Mr. Prader committed a deliberate act of cyber terrorism, an act that could place the lives of Americans citizens and our allies in danger. The case is currently under review and the investigation is in process. We ask that Mr. Prader's family, friends and associates, exercise patience and restraint as we resolve these allegations and bring this matter to a close in as timely manner as possible.*

If they intended to calm the waters, it had the opposite effect. The Independent Movement sprang to action, calling for mass protests in the streets until Freddie was free. Tens of thousands gathered in New York, Boston, Chicago, Philadelphia, Seattle, Portland, San Francisco and Los Angeles. Speaker after speaker stated the case of Freddie Prader as a political prisoner targeted by the NSA and its co-conspirators at Booz Allen for his involvement in the Independent Movement.

In Portland, Roy Jones emerged from hiding to address the protestors. A roar went up when the crowd realized who he was and what he risked by appearing before them.

You all know the story of Freddie Prader. A concerned citizen, a talented non-violent young man who was called upon to engage in a political movement and he answered that call. We were there because we had answered the call as well. Before then, none of us believed that you could work within the system and affect fundamental change. A man named Roman Mason convinced us we were wrong.

The authorities tried to crush us then. The Democrats and Republicans worked in concert to take us down. The government and their agents in law enforcement conducted a campaign of subversion, committed crimes of violence, vandalism, destruction of private property and, yes, terrorism, in order stop us from participating in the democratic process. They wanted to capture and imprison us as terrorists then. They failed because we got the truth out on the worldwide web. We compelled the mainstream media to recognize the truth and we brought the hard, cold facts to the halls of congress.

In the words of Ronald Reagan, here they go again.

We were there when the FBI raided our work center in Seattle. We know what happened that night and, thanks to Freddie Prader, the entire world knows as well. We know that Freddie Prader is a patriot and those who are responsible for his abduction are traitors to our democracy. Freddie is not alone. There are at least half a dozen political prisoners (hundreds if you count those still detained at Guantanamo Bay) detained by our government for acts of subversion and espionage. But the real subversives are the private contractors who have created a monster, a trillion dollar industry, in the wake of September 11, 2001. Most of our intelligence operations are now in private hands. That is the scandal of the century.

Did we really believe that we could place the most valuable commodity of the modern age in private hands and expect that they would not use it for their own gain?

Hundreds of thousands if not millions of citizens are on the streets of protest today. Many will be beaten and detained. Many will face the batons of police and private security forces. Many will be terrorized with tear gas, water cannons and the brutal tactics of law enforcement, all in the name of order.

But CNN will not cover these events. Their reporters populate Freedom Square in Cairo but not Union Square in Manhattan. The liberal Democratic front at MSNBC will give tertiary coverage from floating blimps in major cities before moving on to the real news, the latest show trial or the debate on immigration in the Senate for a bill that is dead on arrival in the Republican controlled House. Fox will give their usual fair and balanced report and the old school networks will offer the same dismissive coverage.

But all of them will take note of what happened here in Portland because of what happens next.

My name is Roy Jones. I am a fugitive from the law. In a few minutes I will become the latest political prisoner to be detained by our government. I offer myself willingly and peacefully because I believe I can accomplish more behind steel bars than I can behind the bars of oppression. I ask only that you do not forget, that you continue the fight for Freddie, for me and for all political prisoners of this nation.

Fronted by police in riot gear, several suits from the FBI pushed through the crowd. Roy instructed them not to resist. He stood and continued speaking until the agents arrived at the stage, handcuffed him and took him away.

Free Freddie! Free Roy! Free Freddie! Free Roy!

Amy watched the local television coverage from a motel room on the outskirts of town, her eyes filled with tears as they hauled her lover away. She supported his decision but not without doubt and regret. Now she faced the possibility that she would not see him again for a very long time. She had recruited him to the cause and she could not but feel responsible. She would deal with the internal struggle the best way she knew how: by moving forward.

Knowing that the authorities would clamp down hard on the Portland activist community, she had to get out of town. She got in her car, an older model Honda supplied by her friends and colleagues, cleared her mind, and drove south. She had enough hard cash not to worry about being tracked. She was off the grid.

She turned off the interstate and headed for the coastal highway. She wanted to gaze at the power and the grace of nature as only the Pacific Ocean could reveal. Its ancient stone monuments rose from the North American continent where it dove to unknown depths. She needed time to think and plan and wonder. She wanted to understand what had happened and what was still happening. She wanted to forgive and be forgiven. Only the ocean in its infinite wisdom could ease the fear that seized her soul.

What happens next? She did not know.

She drove to the little college town of Arcata on the northern California coast, found a tourist motel on the beach and settled in for at least a few days. She would sleep for twelve hours and dream of better days and simpler times. When she awoke, maybe she would know, maybe she would understand.

THE INVITATION

House of Usher
Bishops, Knights & Pawns
The Players' Lounge

It arrived by courier, delivered by a well-coifed man in what could only pass for a uniform because of the hat, reminiscent of those worn by police officers in the fifties and sixties. He handed Rome the invitation and informed him that he would wait for the reply. Accustomed to serving an elite clientele, when invited inside he replied that he would prefer to remain outside. When asked how long he was prepared to wait, he said: As long as it takes, sir.

The invitation beckoned him to a dinner party at Hohenzollern Castle, 50 kilometers south of Stuttgart, Germany, on the occasion of the anniversary of the assassination of Archduke Franz Ferdinand and the Treaty of Versailles, 28 June 1914 and 1919 respectively. It bore the signature of Prince Georg Friedrich, heir to the House of Hohenzollern. He laughed upon reading. It left no time to prepare. He accepted nevertheless and within the hour he sat reading an onboard magazine about the castle, its history and the royal house that claimed it as its own. Standing atop Mount

Hohenzollern, with a spectacular view of the hinterland and the Alps beyond, the castle dated back to the eleventh century. Destroyed in war, its second version stood from 1454 to 1798 when it crumbled into ruins, only the chapel of Saint Michael surviving. The castle today stands as a Neo-Gothic wonder created under the direction of Frederick William the Fourth.

Everything seemed calculated to impress: the arrangements, the chauffeur from the airport, his personal tour of the castle, from its expansive gardens and its carved courtyards, to its halls and show rooms filled with relics and archives, from its magnificent throne room to its stupefying view. It transported him to an ancient world where empires and monarchs and royal families existed not as characters and events in books and fairy tales but as living history. Entering the royal dining hall on the upper floors, his eyes drawn to the southern expanse far, far below, he imagined an enemy army laying siege, the lord of the castle gazing down upon them, beyond their reach, smiling at the futility.

Welcome, Mr. Mason.

Prince Georg extended his hand with a comfortable smile. Dressed in a smart blue business suit, he wore none of the trappings of royalty. Rome shook hands but hesitated, not knowing how to address a crown prince.

Please, call me Georg. I've heard a great deal about you.

Have you?

Indeed. You've been quite the topic of discussion.

It is a rare pleasure to meet you.

Rare though it might have been, the sentiment lacked sincerity and the prince seemed to know it. Rome did not share the fascination of most Americans for royal families and antiquated institutions like monarchy, aristocracy and hereditary succession.

With your permission, we are about to begin the proceedings. You have an assigned seat. I sincerely hope you find your visit both intriguing and gratifying.

He located his seat at the far end of the table from where the prince sat in his figurative throne. They enjoyed a four-course dinner that consumed the better part of three hours. The food and the wine were beyond exquisite, the best he had ever experienced. He engaged those around him in lively discussion: political theory, economics, trade policy and foreign affairs. By and large he found his fellow diners, bankers and businessmen for the most part, educated, well informed and progressive. They believed in closing the gap dividing the elite from the working poor. They believed in alleviating the problem of global warming. They believed in renewable energies, fair trade and the universality of human rights. They believed in the right to medical care and living wages. They believed that those blessed with wealth like they had been should willingly contribute to the well being of society at large. The conservatives in the group tended to mutter incomprehensibly, as if possessing little confidence in their positions or philosophies.

Prince Georg raised his hands and the throng dutifully tapped their wine glasses with their forks for effect. It seemed to Rome artificial and rehearsed so he decided to refrain for now from joining the chorus line.

We are here to commemorate the assassination of one of our own, the Archduke Franz Ferdinand, Royal Prince of Hungary and Bohemia and heir to the Austro-Hungarian throne until his untimely demise. We commemorate as well the Treaty of Versailles. The former led to the world's first global war and the latter all but guaranteed the second. The world will long remember the devastating loss of life, the endless suffering, the shameful waste of resources, the destruction of antiquities and architecture and priceless works of art. Yet those of us gathered here (well, most of us) also know that these cataclysmic events provided a rare opportunity for the redistribution of wealth and power. The wheat and the chaff, the cream rises, the superior man emerges from mass destruction. And so we remember these events with deepest sympathy for humankind and yet we also remember with a quiet sense of gratitude for the new world order that emerged: the rise of the Phoenix!

He raised his glass of red wine and waited as the man seated to his right began a ritual toast to the royal families, the elite, the chosen – the illuminati if you will. They would announce a royal house in sets of three: The House of Rothschild! The House of Du Pont! The House Windsor! Then the diners would call out in unison: Here, here! And they would drink. The waiters immediately refilled glasses and the ritual proceeded: The House of Carnegie! The House of Rockefeller! The House of Stuart! And they drank. The ritual continued until it came to Rome, the third of his set: The House of Vanderbilt! The House of Morgan! Rome hesitated. Sensing the test of his character or his willingness to go along, even in an exercise of theater, he chose an answer that he hoped would balance the two: The House of Usher!

You would have thought a bomb exploded outside the castle walls. For this well-read audience the Edgar Allan Poe tale of madness and the House of Usher's final demise ran in direct conflict with the theme of a rising aristocracy. Was he charging them with madness and predicting their own demise? All eyes turned to their leader, Prince Georg, who smiled broadly, laughed and cheered: Here, here! They drank, the spell broken, tension abated. Yet Rome had distinguished himself in a room where every individual considered himself exceptional. That sense of distinction would survive long after the evening concluded. Many of the men (there were no women) would be stricken with an unfamiliar and disturbing sickness: jealousy. When the House of Usher fell, who would survive to pick up the pieces? Or would it disintegrate as the story implied?

The dinner officially concluded, they moved to an adjoining sitting room, where Rome realized that the party had divided into those who would associate with him and those who would not. He walked through the magnificent room adorned with curtains and tapestry from the fourteenth century and watched the parting of the sea, separating the wheat from the chaff. He admired the classic artwork, busts and drawings by daVinci, sculptures by Donatello, paintings by Fra Angelico and Jan van Eyck. He was stricken by what appeared to be the original Primavera by Botticelli: a depiction of the heavenly beings Mercury, the Graces, Venus, Flora and Chloris. It made him wonder how it connected, if the people here or rather those who employed them, considered themselves deities. Where did he fit in? Who was Prince Georg if not Mercury, messenger of the Gods?

The Prince joined him, providing an historical narrative to the artists who created the works and the times in which they lived. Da Vinci lived in a time of upheaval and enlightenment. Raised in a house of stone, the bastard son of a da Vinci, he was fortunate to receive a rudimentary education.

He was once accused of sodomy and acquitted which might explain his fascination with religious subjects. Then again, he had to make a living. It seems all geniuses do: Da Vinci, Donatello, Botticelli. The church had money and recognized his talent.

If they only knew…

They knew. They empowered him and he empowered them. He gave them a certain knowledge of the future and they used that knowledge to prepare.

Rome slept well if not long. He dreamed of the fourteenth century, a castle under siege. He was not in the castle but among the foot soldiers laboring to climb the mountain while cannon roared and soldiers died. He walked out to the balcony and contemplated the events of the last twenty-four hours. He came to a number of conclusions and one critical observation: the castle had no technology, no electronic communication devices, no televisions, no computers and no cell phones except in the lobby where tourists paid for their guided tours. The castle's isolation and thick stone walls meant that it could not be monitored. It was off the grid. Nothing that happened here could be recorded.

He watched the morning fog rise in the hinterlands until it surrounded the castle and he realized that was how they did it, how they captured the castle. They advanced under the cover of the forest and, then, under the cover of the morning fog, they closed to the castle walls.

When the castle and its inhabitants had stirred from their slumber, a servant delivered a light breakfast, coffee, bacon and croissants, along with several newspapers: The London Times, The Guardian, The Washington Post and USA Today. He laughed at that.

A PATRIOT DIRGE

The Prince had a distinct sense of humor. Without an itinerary he scoured the news. The Times had a small article in the back pages concerning the ongoing detention of Freddie Prader, the arrest of Roy Jones in Portland and the escape of Amy Goodall. The Post covered the story below the fold on the front page but The Guardian provided extensive coverage, including a photograph of Roman Mason, founder of the American Independent Movement. He did not bother to check USA Today.

Midmorning, Prince Georg summoned him for a one-to-one meeting on the balcony outside his quarters, a space worthy of an heir to his kingdom, a kingdom that no longer existed in the real world.

People tend to describe me as succinct because I don't believe in circumlocution. I believe in saying what you intend to say and doing what you intend to do.

That's fairly circumlocuitous.

So it is. I do enjoy your sense of humor. I find it is important in a working relationship.

Agreed.

Your colleagues, Mr. Jones and Mr. Prader, will be released by the time you return to American soil. It was all a misunderstanding, an error in judgment on the part of certain overzealous law enforcement officials.

I'm pleased to hear it.

The Prince was a handsome man with an engaging smile and a pleasant personality. He seemed determined to avoid conflict if possible and given his status and influence, his warmth and sincerity (or its appearance) surprised Rome. On those occasions when he had encountered royalty before, the airs of protocol and privilege precluded any chance of true communication.

I understand you are a master chess player.

I enjoy the game but I'm no master.

In any case, you understand the game. You know for example the most powerful and important piece on the board.

A fool's challenge: The Queen is by far the most powerful piece but her entire function is to protect the King, the all-important piece.

Of course, you can lose your Queen and still win but you cannot lose your King. The game is a fitting metaphor for life. There are roughly seven billion people on the planet and all but a few thousand will never advance beyond the experience of pawns. They create their own divisions of influence that allow them to feel meaningful but they are eminently replaceable. You, sir, have an opportunity to advance. The individuals at last evening's dinner can be considered Bishops and Knights. I fancy myself a Castle. If you accept our proposal, you can join them on terms you will find to your liking. The vast majority of these men and women like them (yes, there are women) have reached the pinnacle of their ambitions but some will have the opportunity to advance further. I believe you are among the latter.

Rome processed his words and searched through layers of meaning and intent, seeking a hidden message or a revelation.

What you experienced last evening, as you might have gathered, was a charade, a ritual designed purely for the enjoyment of the participants. There is no aristocracy. There is no New World Order per se. The mythology of thirteen families ruling the world in perpetuity by right of hereditary succession is just that. Mythology. I apologize for not letting you in on the protocol. Frankly, we wanted to see how you'd respond. Your response exceeded our expectations. We need people who will break the mold. We need creative minds with the ability to foresee events and prepare accordingly.

What is your proposal?

The Prince waited, as if calculating how much to reveal and how much to keep hidden. Could he trust this newcomer, this self-styled revolutionary, this dissident voice determined to achieve fundamental change in American politics? Rome watched and recognized the calculation but offered no assurances.

We are philanthropists. We have always been the world's leading philanthropists. We want you to create a foundation for the cause of your choosing: Global warming, international rights of labor, fair trade policy, world hunger, disease, poverty -- virtually anything with the exception of electoral politics. You will have absolute control and all the resources you require. You will be able to do more good for more people than you could ever have dreamed.

His mind raced through the possibilities of what could be accomplished with unlimited funds. How could he resist? Was this the price of compromising your soul and, if it was, was it worth it? All this for doing what he had already agreed to do. Clearly, they doubted his sincerity.

Anything but electoral politics?

Yes. That you must leave to your colleagues.

You will not impede them?

I cannot guarantee that some of the organizations we support will not engage in what is commonly known as dirty politics. I can guarantee that there will be no violence, no threats and no further acts of extortion. Not under our authority in any case. One cannot account for the actions of an overzealous administrator but one can correct the error.

They tried to read each other, to understand each other as potential adversaries or friends. Pieces moved across the board, pawns sacrificed for position, clearing pathways of attack. So many questions remained that could not be answered, an opening, a setting of the stage. Did he expect an answer today, tomorrow, next week or next year?

Limitations and conditions?

Yes. For example, should you choose to advance the cause of alternative energies, we would not be willing to rebuild the entire infrastructure of Europe or America. But we would be willing to help you create a model to demonstrate the economic viability of such a project. We could for example affect the rebuilding California's infrastructure. Of course, it would require government cooperation and that is within our sphere of influence.

Universal mass transit and solar panels on every roof?

It is a reasonable goal.

I am reasonably impressed. When do you expect an answer?

Soon.

What's the hurry?

There is none.

Give me a week.

The Prince refilled his coffee, gazed out at the magnificent landscape, and wondered at Rome's request. Was it his well-known need for contemplation or something else? Did he need a week to plan some nefarious action? No matter. He would be under constant surveillance.

Very well. You will be provided a secure email address. Contact us when you are ready to talk.

With your permission, I'll make my own return travel arrangements.

Another interesting request. No matter. Their eyes and ears were everywhere. He would find nowhere to hide.

Certainly. One last thing: Your organization does not concern us. It is a nuisance. That is all. It is you we are interested in. If you accept our proposition, you will gain a place at the table. Isn't that what you've always wanted?

The question made Rome uncomfortable. They knew far more about him than they should have known. Isn't that what he wanted? Isn't that what his father before him wanted? How could he refuse? And yet, an uncomfortable feeling remained. What was it he said about da Vinci? They empowered him so that he could empower them.

He took a ride to the airport and booked passage for London.

MAGGIE'S DILEMMA

A Caged Animal
Going Public
Puzzle Pieces

She felt cornered, trapped and isolated by the course of events. Like a caged animal she had no way out and no one to whom she could turn for help. She had been unable to contact Rome since he informed her of the decision to disband the core group. She argued against it but in the end he wore her down. She could no more risk the lives of others than he could. But there had to be another way.

She wanted to go public with the information they had. An unknown person or persons made a threat and made good on that threat, endangering the life a child. If they went public, she argued, they would be protected. Any further acts of violence, any deaths or sudden disappearances under curious circumstance, would at the least be subject to scrutiny, including the possibility of congressional inquiry. He replied that they had already gone public by posting the email. They had created a public record. He asked her to have faith that the movement would survive without its core leadership.

They will find their own leaders and emerge stronger

than ever.

She hoped he was right but that was before Freddie and Roy were detained. Now Amy was on the run and Rome had vanished. She contacted everyone with a connection to him but no one knew anything, not even Sinclair. It struck her odd that Sinclair did not sound alarmed. He expressed concern but advised patience. When she asked if he had gone to the cabin, he avoided a direct answer, suggesting instead that his mental state was healthy. What did he know that he would not reveal? He almost seemed to be talking in puzzles, abstractions, something about unplanned journeys and unknown ambitions, as if someone was listening or watching who could not be trusted.

She needed to act. To be in a position to do something and to watch while her friends and loved ones suffered, while her lover, the only man she would ever love, seemed to have vanished without a word of warning, would be unconscionable. She asked Sinclair twice if he had gone to the cabin. No, he finally said. No.

As the leader of the Independent caucus, she demanded a hearing and went public: In a matter of days, the founder of the Independent Movement had declared the core leadership group disbanded, two of their core members had been detained on phony terrorist charges, an anonymous threat had been made and now, the founder himself had disappeared. The Independent Movement had already been targeted by the authorities and had been vindicated. The endemic corruption of the major parties, their complicity in criminal activities, had been exposed for all to see. Had we forgotten so soon?

The moment she went public the hammer came

slamming down and the whip came snapping in the form of the Democratic Party whip. She had worked with him. Despite their differences and party affiliations, she regarded him with respect. On this occasion he sent his aide, meaning he did not want to be accountable.

I've come as a friend.

Whenever politicians begin with that sentiment what follows is anything but friendly. I come as a friend: Your spouse has accused you of infidelity. I come as a friend: Your name came up in a corruption scandal. I come as a friend: If you don't stand down, your dog will be lost and your best friend homeless. A preamble to impending doom or a thinly veiled warning, in her experience politicos never came as a friend.

We have deep sympathy for what's happened to your colleagues. It's not right. It's unjust. It should be investigated.

She appeared attentive and engaged, a practiced response, a pose, a mask, while her mind remained focused on Rome, wondering if this intervention would have any bearing on the problem at hand.

However, if you hadn't gone to the press, the problem might have been resolved by now. We have information that Mr. Prader and Mr. Jones were about to be released when this story broke.

She wanted to say: What story? She had said nothing that was not already known. She had only forced the media to address it. She had deliberately withheld the attack on the child, not wanting to endanger the child's family. Miguel Estrada had contacted her to make that request and she honored it.

He shrugged.

Water under the bridge. Damage done.

How politicians and their underlings loved clichés. They used them, abused them, tucked them away and resurrected them, one for every occasion, even in their private conversations. Under normal circumstances, it bored her but now it crawled under her skin and she worried that she could no longer hold her true thoughts in check.

The thing is: It's not too late. If you'll agree to stand down, no press conferences, no congressional inquiry, they could be released tomorrow. No charges, no recriminations, just a little misunderstanding.

That's fine but Freddie and Roy are not the only ones involved in this affair.

All charges will be dropped against Amy Goodall.

Roman Mason is missing.

He's fine. He's in London. He should have contacted you by now.

She should have been relieved and below the surface she was but anger born of frustration rushed from her heart and spoke before her mind could retrieve it.

How in the world would you know where Rome is?

He squirmed with discomfort on the other side of her desk. He did not relish this kind of task but it came with the job. Maggie sensed that he wanted to be more forthcoming than he should and more than his boss had authorized. She neither encouraged him nor put his worry to rest. She simply waited for his answer.

There are people involved, important people, influential people. I don't know who they are. I don't even know if the congressman does. What I do know is: If we get a call, we jump. I'm sure they have money but it's more than that. We don't jump for Chase Manhattan. We don't jump for BP.

Hell, we don't jump like that for anyone.

He went silent and Maggie tried to determine whether he was pausing for effect or deciding that he'd said enough. She saw him sweat and that alone told her more than anything he had said thus far.

I really don't want any of this getting back to the congressman. He'd fire me quicker than I can answer the phone. The fact is: these people have information.

I understand.

No, you don't. They have information on everyone and everything. That's how we knew Mason was in London.

At last he had given her information of value, something that demanded her attention, and a clue as to why Rome had disbanded the core and ended up in Europe. All pieces of a puzzle are not equal; some reveal surrounding pieces until a greater picture can be envisioned. Now she had to decide what to do about it.

Why did you tell me this?

The nervous man shifted and looked about as if trying to determine whether or not anyone could be listening or watching. He had the look of a man who had said too much, gone too far, and wanted to walk it back before he realized that possibility had evacuated the premises.

I don't know. Some of us actually believe in democracy. I know I do. Maybe you can do something about it. The congressman can't or won't. The Speaker can't or won't. The President can't or won't. Maybe no one can.

She noticed the blinking red light on her phone and answered it. Her secretary conveyed an anonymous cable from London. It read: Rome is fine and wishes you were here. She would have it traced to Kings Place in London, the building that headquartered The Guardian. Another piece of the puzzle revealed.

Rome's fine. He's in London. Are we done here?

Looking like a clerk in a local auto parts store instead of an aide to one of the most powerful members of congress, he nodded and stood on unsteady knees.

You advise the congressman?

Yes.

What would you advise me?

I'd tell you to take the deal. After that you're on your own.

Thank you.

He left her to contemplate the pieces of the puzzle. Rome had recognized the greater enemy and seized the moment. Shifting through possible courses of action, she reached a decision. She canceled her evening press conference and went home early.

SAFE HOUSE

A Mouse Trap
Surveillance State
Reckless and Dangerous

She dyed and styled her hair in the manner of Solange from The Girl with the Dragon Tattoo, completing the look with boots and leather at a local thrift store. She knew her appearance would draw attention, even in the coastal towns that welcomed all but the homeless, but anyone looking for Amy Goodall would look the other way.

Arcata is a college town and every college town on the west coast had an activist community and every activist community had a connection to Amy. She only had to wait, sipping coffee at the Main Street Café on the plaza until someone recognized her and sat down to talk. She sat by the windows reading an essay entitled Infant Nation from a pamphlet in the community reading collection when a young woman in tie-dye and dreadlocks sat down at her table.

You're Amy Goodall.

Amy glanced up, nodded and went back to her reading. The woman spoke just above a whisper and focused her gaze outside.

They've been asking about you on campus. Nobody

knows who they are. No uniforms, no badges. Just people. They show your picture and ask if we've seen you. Nobody has...until now. I've got to tell you: these people are scary.

Amy thanked her, walked to her car and started driving south.

There exists in this world few drives as beautiful as the coastal highway winding like a snake in sand from Tacoma to Mendocino but Amy no longer noticed. She concentrated on the road and the path forward until the sea began to consume the sun. It reawakened her sense of wonder and she pulled off the highway before the highway pulled her over the edge. She breathed in the sweet saltwater air, tasted the tears of the great Pacific, swallowed the sorrows of life and beheld the immutable power of the vast, undulating waves of the endless sea. She loved the sea. She could not live more than a week without longing for the sea. No matter where she traveled, no matter the pressures and complications, she always found her way back. In her dreams she lived by the sea and in the end she wanted to die there.

Stronger now, steadier on her feet, sharper in her thoughts, she climbed down the embankment and walked the narrow beach, waves of gold and gray moonlight, rolling and crashing in harmony with the beat of her heart. She walked until the palate of her thoughts and emotions cleared and she became aware of the rising tide, waves crashing louder and closer, the walkway of sand beneath the rocky wall narrowing. A part of her wanted to make a stand here and now, testing the fates, allowing the sea to take her into her vast arms, sweeping her away to freedom and peace. Salty tears welled in her eyes and she realized she could not abandon her cause and her friends in a time of need.

She climbed the wall, slipping as she went, struggling to reach the safety of the walking path above. She noticed in the corner of her mind a car parked a good distance from where she had parked. She made a point not to look. Was she being followed? Or had paranoia crept back into her consciousness? Act natural. Walk back to the car. Don't look back. If they wanted to take her, they had her. Why hadn't they? Why wouldn't they? Of course. Why take one when you take them all? She would lead them to others and everyone she contacted would be guilty of aiding a fugitive. Like the old Russian gulag, they wanted to round them all up and put them away, silence them, destroy them.

She drove on, one eye in the rear mirror, slowing to see her pursuer pull onto the road just as she neared a curve. Doubt slipped away like time to a dying man. She slowed until she could see his face in the gray moonlight: a typical thirty something foot soldier in the war on civil liberties, pale but not too pale, neither handsome nor ugly, his features cried out anonymity. He stayed at a reasonable distance behind her, understanding that he'd been made, not knowing what followed. She slowed again to test his intentions, forcing him to commit, pressing him to act. His mouth moved as if talking to an invisible companion, updating his superior, asking for advise or taking orders. The thin line of a crooked smile emerged from his face as he eased forward on the accelerator. The front bumper of his car, a late model Audi, pressed against her rear bumper. Instinctively, she increased her speed and he followed.

Having passed Mendocino on her way to Port

Arena, the highway straightened for the most part, departing from the coastal cliffs to grassland and thick pine forests. Amy knew this road; she had traveled it many times and she wondered as she pressed down on the accelerator how well her pursuer knew it. He stayed with her like the tail of a cat bobbing and weaving down the highway. He nearly lost control at a dangerous turn as she sprinted ahead, cars and trucks honking their alarm.

She had to decide whether to continue on the coast highway or take the 128 through the coastal range. Either way would challenge the best of drivers. Either way could mean the end for anyone foolish enough to test the limits. Taking the coast route would require coming to a near stop so, at the very last second, she chose the inland route and braced for the chase. If he wanted to play, she would give him the challenge he desired. The road ran along the Navarro River. She floored for the straightaway before the path began to wind through the towering redwoods. She banked into the first hard curve and her pursuer fell back. Whirring past a car traveling at a reasonable speed, she felt a surge of confidence. The chaser didn't know the road or maybe he had just wanted to give her a scare. A logging truck sounded its horn and she eased up just in time to slip past. Rule of the road: Where there's one logging truck, there's usually another. Glancing in the rearview, she saw the chaser still there, gaining ground, and she had to wonder what his intentions.

If she pulled over and stopped, would he arrest her, take her into custody, drive her to San Francisco and hand her over to the FBI? Or would she become the first casualty in the war on the Independence Movement? Who was he? Who did he work for? If he caught up to her, would he drive her off the road?

They were playing a dangerous game and the deeper they got into the forest, the more dangerous it became. The road narrowed and wound through the silver forest back and forth, back and forth, and she kept up her speed, trying to maintain a safe distance but the gap between them closed. They climbed the mountain turn after harrowing turn, passing cars and trucks, inviting disaster and the chaser did not relent. She skidded on the gravel surface of a turnout and barely held on. They increased their speed on every stretch of straight roadway, testing the limits like adolescents who believe in their own immortality. She heard the sound of a trucker's horn just as she passed a car.

She pulled over at the next turnout, exhausted, unable to move, petrified. What flows through the mind at the moment death's fingers brush your cheek? Do you see the events of your life in a flood of images? Do you see what might have been? Or is it only pavement and trees, tires screeching and the crunch of metal bombarding your senses in their last breath? Amy saw Roy, his manner calm, his face unruffled as the FBI handcuffed and shuffled him away. She slowed her breathing and calmed her pounding heart. What happened? Was it still happening? She walked back to the scene of destruction. The truck had fishtailed, hoisting its haul of logs across the road. The cab managed to stay upright, the driver talking on his cell, summoning assistance. The car she had passed somehow managed to escape harm but the Audi lay crushed under a maze of logs down the roadside embankment. She saw no motion, heard no cry for help. She started down the slope but the trucker grabbed her arm.

Them logs is unstable. No use two folks dying.

She looked at the logger and back down at the crushed vehicle. She wondered what the Audi driver would do in her place. Was he a killer or a fool? Would he have checked to make sure she was dead before driving off, a job well done? She would never know.

Helps a coming. Nothing more you can do here, m'am. Might as well be on your way.

She took the trucker's advice, driving through the night until she reached Santa Rosa. She paid for a motel room and had a meal at an all-night diner, all the while sifting through events, putting the pieces together. This did not smell like the FBI or Homeland Security. The government would not be so reckless. It didn't feel like party operatives. They could be reckless but they showed some restraint before resorting to acts of violence. In late night ramblings fueled by bountiful quantities of wine Rome often speculated about the hidden rulers, the corporate elite, the illuminati, the overlords, those who reined in shadows over CEO's, bankers and heads of government. No one took his midnight musings born of wine and spirits seriously but now, after the anonymous warning, the endangerment of a child and an attempt on her own life, the time to reconsider had arrived.

She had to make contact with her colleagues in the organization. After a night of too much thought and too little sleep, she waited until after the morning rush of traffic and drove into Berkeley. They had a safe house on Dana Street, a small, beige duplex with turquoise trim. They held on to it as they had a number of others in strategic cities in the event things went bad and they were unable once again to operate as a public organization. She parked in a garage not far from the university, took a stroll down Telegraph for old times, and made her way to the Dana Street duplex, making sure no one had followed. The safe house used a signal to indicate a warning. A silver star in the second story window meant all was well. A peace symbol meant the opposite. Walking on the other side of the street, she glanced up to see the silver star. She continued walking around the block, came back, and knocked on the door. She knew the woman who opened the door and smiled. She was a friend.

Can I help you?

Is Julian here?

No, he left for the day.

Thanks. I'll come back this evening.

She turned and walked through the alley to Haste Street, glancing behind to see two men emerge from the safe house, guns drawn.

Homeland Security! Halt!

Taking a chance they wouldn't fire in the middle of a crowed city, she dashed into a child development center where she watched them split up, one going east and the other west. She waited and went back to the safe house where her friend and colleague waved her to her car. Amy got in and they drove toward the highway and the Bay Bridge.

How long have they been here?

Two days.

How did they know? How did they know about the star?

I don't know, Amy. They know everything.

Did they tag your car?

I don't know. Probably.

We'll have to ditch it in San Francisco.

A PATRIOT DIRGE

She had one last chance: the safe house in San Francisco. Unlike the house in Berkeley, it had no electronic communication devices; no cell phones, no land phones and no computers allowed. The address was delivered in written form only with instructions to burn it immediately. If a member was pressured, they had a decoy. If the decoy was closed, they set up another. If they (whomever they were) knew about the Joplin house on Haight Street, she had no recourse. She would turn herself in.

They negotiated the maze before rush hour and drove across the Bay Bridge, a one-time marvel of engineering until the 1989 earthquake knocked it down. A newer, better bridge had been forged in China with Chinese workers and Chinese steel. If this could happen in San Francisco what hope did we have for the rest of the nation? They parked the car in a lot off Mission, took a cab to Haight and Ashbury, and walked several blocks to where Cole ends at Haight. Walking along the other side of the street, Amy glanced up at the posters in the bay windows of the corner three-story building: Jerry Garcia, Jim Morrison and Janis Joplin. You could hear her sing Ball and Chain every time you saw it.

They lingered at some storefront windows catering to old-time hippies and tourists alike. Then they doubled back to the Red Victorian, across the street from the Joplin House, sat at the windows, ordered lunch and watched the street life for close to an hour. Everything seemed normal. Locals walked to their destinations, tourists gaping with their shopping bags, the occasional homeless person and drug dealer. The Haight had cleaned up its act but remnants of the old days remained. Finally, Amy rose and whispered to her friend: *Stay here.* She walked out of the café and walked halfway across Haight when at least seven men in FBI uniforms emerged from various vehicles and hiding places and converged on her.

They cuffed her as one man read her rights and escorted her to a waiting van. The last thing she heard before they closed the van's rear doors was her friend's voice: *I'm sorry, Amy! They have my grandmother!*

Who were these people and what was their game?

OFF THE GRID

Subterfuge
International Connections
Tapping the Free Press

Certain that the Prince would have him followed, convinced that the organization's surveillance depended on electronic communications, financial transactions, emails and phone calls, Rome planned his escape meticulously. He had numerous international connections in both the business and activist worlds but few he could trust with his life or the lives of those he loved. One maintained residencies in Amsterdam and the south of France. A Parisian by birth, Marcel Rochelle had earned his fortune much as Rome had, buying low and selling high, and now he lived a life of leisure. Rome had on occasion visited him in Amsterdam and knew he preferred the northern clime in the summer months.

The Prince's limousine provided him a ride from the castle to the airport, where he asked the driver to wait while he transformed his credit card into Euros. He insisted on providing a generous tip and watched him drive away, passing the overnight parking lot with a glance in the rearview mirror. If the driver had instructions to keep him under watch, at least until he boarded his plane, as Rome suspected he did, he now had the burden of exiting the airport and returning to the overnight lot.

He purchased a first class ticket to London and proceeded through the security gate for international travelers. In the boarding lounge, where non-ticket holders could not roam, he sat beside an older man sporting a full beard and dressed in clothing similar to his own. The man had a placard with a double-digit number on it, indicating he had no assurance of boarding the plane in question unless a certain number of cancellations occurred. He engaged the man in casual conversation, learning that he had traveled to Stuttgart on business and did not relish the idea of waiting in the airport before returning home. Rome offered a trade, explaining that he had yet another matter that needed his attention before boarding the scheduled flight. The man gratefully accepted and he walked out of the terminal, hailing a cab to the local bus station.

Using his fresh supply of Euros, he boarded a bus for Frankfurt, took a stroll on the River Main and enjoyed a light lunch. He then boarded a bus for Düsseldorf where he lodged at a modest motel. He took a cab to the nearest public library where he paid a young man five euros for the use of his computer time. Running a search for prominent international bankers, chief executive officers and leading administrators in the world of international finance, he identified a dozen individuals who had attended the gathering at the castle. Without comment he emailed their pictures along with a Google search of Castles in Europe (with Hohenzollern highlighted) to an email account set up for anonymity. He could only hope that Freddie's security measures held.

The subject: Wish U Were Here.

He found much of the city charming, with narrow cobblestone streets, its outdoor marketplaces and quaint shops. A mostly modern city, it protected its older neighborhoods, its trees and parks, while catering to corporate interests with more than an ample supply of high-rise offices and modern shopping centers. He could see that what was happening here was happening all over Europe: a transformation in the corporate image of America. If old neighborhoods, museums and ancient architecture stood in the way of profit, they had to go. Industrialization, finance, technology, compartmentalization, cheap labor, these would rule the future while art and aesthetics declined. Soon, a people's history would reach back no further than a few months, unless a greater interest, an elite, a superior class (if you will) found reason to hang on to events like September 11, 2001.

In the morning he boarded a train for Amsterdam, a high-speed railway that transported him from the plush green flatlands of northern Germany to the city of a thousand canals, one of the great artistic capitals of the world. If there existed a foundation on which other cities should be modeled it would be Amsterdam. If there existed a nation to the same purpose it might well be The Netherlands. Of course, even Holland had witnessed a great deal of change. Faced with the real threat of Islamic extremist terrorism, a threat that struck at the heart of the city with the assassination of Theo van Gogh, the reactionary right had gained ground in national politics. It remained to be seen how long Amsterdam's famed liberalism would survive.

He booked a room at the Hotel Beursstraat, enjoyed

lunch at the Café De Deugniet, and walked to 133 Oudezijds Voorburgwal, a four story building adorned with full sized statues of robed goddesses and the summer home of Marcel Rochelle. His ruffled appearance startled the woman who answered the door. He carried only a small travel bag and had worn the same clothing, a fine but now wrinkled suit provided by the Prince, since he left the castle. He had neglected to trim his beard and now that he thought of it, he might have forgotten to comb his hair. When he asked for Marcel she hesitated.

Tell him Rome is calling.

Through the double doors at the street-level entryway, he heard her footsteps climbing the stairs and momentarily a heavier set descending. Marcel emerged on the second story balcony: *Monsieur Mason! So good to see you!* He continued his descent, opening the double doors and waving his friend inside. His female companion, having followed him down the stairs, kept her distance as if uncertain of her role or the relative safety of their strange visitor.

What brings you to Amsterdam, my friend?

Business, I'm afraid.

Pity! You look as though you could use some rest and relaxation.

I apologize for my appearance. I'll attend to it shortly.

No need.

I've come to you in confidence.

Marcel glanced back at his companion, motioning her to come.

This is my friend, Mademoiselle Cherie. She was just telling me she has some important shopping to do. Cherie promptly grabbed her purse and departed with a curtsy: *Very pleased to meet you, monsieur.*

Marcel led him to his study on the third floor and closed the door behind them. The room served as a vessel for exquisite red velvet and carved hardwood furnishings, its walls graced with extraordinary drawings and paintings, including several by van Gogh. He sat behind his mahogany desk and assumed the posture of a man about to be engaged in business. Rome strolled to the glass balcony doors, gazing at the street life below, and began his account in some detail of the event at Hohenzollern Castle from the moment of his sudden departure in Seattle to his personal invitation to join the organization as the head of a philanthropic endeavor by the Prince himself. He turned to observe an expression of concern but not surprise on the face of his friend.

Forgive me, monsieur, but I do not know how I might help in this matter. At first look it would seem an opportunity to do great good. Is that not what you have always desired?

One would think.

Did you accept the proposition?

I asked for seven days, during which I found it desirable if not necessary to secure some measure of privacy, anonymity if you will. Toward that end, I am unable to communicate with my friends and colleagues in the States by traditional means. That's where I need your assistance.

Of course, my friend, it is little to ask. What would you have me communicate?

Rome gave instructions to wait twenty-four hours and then cable the office of Representative Margaret Thomas from an anonymous associate in London with the message that he is fine. He asked Marcel to contact John Sinclair in Seattle with the same message and an additional reference to an article in The Guardian concerning their common acquaintances. He asked him to contact the Prince, if possible, to relay the message that he would consider his proposition only if his colleagues had been released.

Marcel wrote it all down carefully and asked if there was anything else he could do to help, an alternative identity and passport perhaps? Rome declined.

You will have done enough. If the Prince pressures you for information, please tell him everything you know. We have nothing to hide.

Very well, monsieur, it is a pleasure as always.

They shook hands and Rome departed. Marcel watched him from the balcony until he crossed the canal and disappeared. Then, he picked up the phone.

WISH U WERE HERE

Last Man Standing
Master Player
Secrets and Diversions

Sinclair felt like the last player chosen, destined to sit on the bench watching others engage in a competition. A man in a box, stymied and isolated, he waited for an opportunity that arrived in the form of a puzzle: an email to a secret account, an account in theory accessible only to him and a select few in a tight circle of trusted individuals. Most would be unable to receive the message due their circumstance.

Amy was on the run and could not risk electronic communications. Freddie and Roy remained in custody despite rumors of their imminent release. Maggie, as a member of congress, did not engage in such clandestine matters. Sara Kent had instructions to remain outside the group's operations and Miguel Estrada chose to do the same. Rome had either vanished or, as Sinclair considered a certainty, had sent the message from an unknown location in Europe.

With the group's consent, Freddie had given access to no more than two or three anonymous individuals as a failsafe. Beyond them, Sinclair was the last man standing. It fell to him to collect the pieces and construct them into a coherent picture. He relished the role. Finally, he had received the call to abandon his place on the sidelines and get in the game.

It did not take long to identify the dignitaries of international finance and extrapolate dozens more as likely associates. He knew many of them. He had walked the same path, inhabited the same boardrooms, attended the same smoke rooms and dining halls until his career and interests diverged. They did not as a rule take an interest in politics except as fodder for conversation. They paid others to ensure that politicians, regardless of party or philosophy, served their financial interests.

The Castles of Europe brought a smile to his face. As a young man, his father, a man of vast inherited wealth, told him a story of being whisked away in the middle of the night and attending a dinner of very powerful men at a castle somewhere in Europe. His father used the term: Illuminati. He had never heard that word before his father spoke it and, even then, especially then, it carried a connotation of secrecy and danger. Sinclair had related the story to Rome in one of their midnight musings. In his experience, everything, however distant or remote, comes back around to complete the circle, and events that seemed random or irrelevant emerge without warning as critical clues.

He had a white board across one wall of his study and he began to construct the organizational structure of the overlords on one half and a map of the prominent castles of Europe on the other. The picture grew clearer. The great unknown and therefore the first objective of their endeavor was to reveal the identities of the overlords themselves. He deduced that Rome had attended a gathering of high-level administrators in the organization. Like his father, he had been asked to join them. His father, not particularly interested in philanthropic enterprise, had declined. What had Rome decided? Why had he disappeared? Had he gone underground or had he been eliminated? It seemed to Sinclair that Rome surely would have accepted the offer as a means to infiltrate the organization. The only logical conclusion was that he had delayed his decision in order to buy time and make necessary preparations.

He had referenced an article in The Guardian. Why? Sinclair had read the article several times. The writer had a clear grasp of the facts and used them to level an effective indictment of the American government's assault on civil liberties in the name of the war on terror. He did not, however, reveal anything Sinclair did not already know. If the article contained any hidden clues or coded messages, it escaped his ability to perceive them.

He googled The Guardian in London and then it struck him like a shock to the central nervous system: Kings Place not only housed The Guardian but also one of Europe's most prominent internet technology corporations. Logica had recently been sold to a Canadian based company, Information Systems and Management Consultants, for nearly two billion dollars. Rome did not believe in coincidence and neither did Sinclair.

The reference was not simply a suggestion for getting the story to the press; it was a warning that the press could not be trusted. Even the liberal press and those journalists who presented themselves as champions of civil liberty could not be trusted. They received not only their money from the corporate elites;

they received their information from them as well.

Sinclair marveled at the mystery that appeared before him and wondered what direction Rome had gone with this information. Did he have a plan? What did he expect of others? What kind of assistance did he need? He had done what he could: Analysis, inference and deduction. He had drawn the pieces together in a logical manner.

Next, he needed to get the information and analysis to someone who could act. For the first time, he tapped the emergency email Freddie had provided each of them before his detention. The response came in the form of a ticket to a Seattle Mariners game delivered by courier on a bicycle. He enjoyed baseball, a game of numbers, a slow paced thinking man's game, but he resented having to perform on the field. He considered himself a brain, a big brain, a director who orchestrated tableaus and delivered orders to actors and technicians but never ever took the stage. He understood, however, that all the actors were unavailable.

He transferred the organizational chart and his rendering of the castles of Europe to paper and erased his whiteboard before changing his attire and catching a cab to Safeco Field. He purchased a program and located his seat, a premium location at field level on the first base side. King Felix, the finest pitcher in a Mariners' uniform since Gaylord Perry, took the mound against an upstart Oakland Athletics team. It promised to be an excellent game. For three innings he sat watching a pitcher's dual, the seat to his left as empty as a homeless man's bank account. Finally, a young man with a patchy beard, carrying popcorn and a beer sat beside him and spoke.

Don't look at me.

My apologies. I'm new at this.
You're being followed.
Christ! I knew this was a bad idea.

He started to look back and the young man cautioned him.

Watch the game.

He did. The young Oakland pitcher proved to be an effective combination of guile and talent, carving the strike zone like a seasoned veteran. The teams matched zeroes into the fifth inning. He almost forgot his purpose and the young man sitting next to him.

What do you know?

I have an organizational chart and a rendering of European castles most likely to host gatherings.

Excellent. After the last pitch, leave it in your seat.

They watched the game. After seven innings both pitchers had surrendered a single run and their pitch counts ran over a hundred and ten. The Oakland pitcher went down first and King Felix thereafter. The game remained a one to one tie.

You should go to London. See the reporter for The Guardian. He's a journalist, a good one. Either way, we'll find out what we need to know.

Oakland drew a walk, stole a base and sacrificed the runner to third. An intentional walk followed by a sacrifice fly and the Mariners were down two to one. The Oakland closer walked a man but retired the side. Game over. He placed his notes on the seat, walked up the stairs and out of the stadium, noticing every face, every set of eyes, that seem to linger on him too long. *Never again,* he said to his self. He flagged a cab, went home and secured first class passage to London at midday following.

INDEFINITE DETENTION

Isolation
Test of Loyalty
What Price Liberty?

They put a hood over his head, tossed him in the back of a van and drove around until his disorientation was complete. They put him in a room without windows, without natural light, with only a single naked bulb overhead. Time had no markers. No one talked to him. No one visited him. No one observed him unless they placed a camera in a crack of the concrete walls. He checked and found nothing. He slept and awakened, exercised and played mental games. They delivered food and water without comment through a slot in the metal door. No schedule, no timetable that he could decipher. Two large buckets and a roll of toilet paper in one corner of the space served as his bathroom. Days after his internment they had not been emptied.

Measuring the days by his internal clock, on the fourth day the door slammed open and a woman, thirtyish and attractive, walked into the room as two men carried in a card table and two folding chairs. In an act of apparent kindness, they removed the buckets and the door clanked shut. She sat in one chair and waited until he sat in the other.

How would you like to go home?

No, thanks, I like it here.

She smiled and took stock of him. He had not bathed, shaved or showered in however many days had passed. It got to the point that he could smell his own body odor and then he couldn't.

We could walk out that door together. You could be in your own home tomorrow.

Tomorrow and tomorrow and tomorrow creeps in this petty pace to the last syllable of recorded time.

We like you, Freddie. We want you to work for us. But it's up to you.

No thanks.

She waited and let the silence settle. She knew he enjoyed her presence, her voice, her smile and her perfume. He took it in, breathed it in, and stored it in great detail for recall at a later time.

Isolation can do strange things to the human mind. Maybe you'll be more receptive tomorrow.

Tomorrow and tomorrow and tomorrow...

She knocked on the door. The two men retrieved the table and chairs, clanging the door shut behind, returning him to his solitary confinement. The next day, after a similar exchange, they cuffed him, hooded him, and escorted him to a car for a twenty-minute ride, leading to a thirty-minute helicopter ride. They placed him on a plane where he flew for about an hour. Another thirty minutes in a ground vehicle and they reached their destination. They pulled him out, walked him inside, took him on an elevator down three floors, and guided him to a room. The removed the cuffs and left.

Freddie removed the hood and looked around at his

new confinement. Larger than his previous space, it had no windows or natural light but it did have chairs, tables and an array of computers, printers and monitors. He sat on the sofa to contemplate the possibilities. Unlike his previous accommodations this one had a toilet and sink behind a temporary barrier. The blessings of modern plumbing had never been so poignant. He didn't need to look for cameras and microphones; they were clearly placed in every corner of the room, including the makeshift bathroom.

It seemed clear what they intended. They wanted him to engage the world through their computers. They would defy him to try to find a way around their monitoring devices. They wanted him to contact his friends in the internet community. They wanted him to contact his colleagues in the Independence Movement. They wanted him to open the door to Anonymous. If he cooperated, to the extent he cooperated, they would make his life more comfortable. His instinct told him to take the challenge. He could outsmart them. Get on the web and run them through a maze. Lead them into a black hole or take them down a tunnel of a thousand decoys. He owned the web.

But they owned the playground. They wanted him to think he could outplay them on their own field with their set of rules, rules that no one knew but them. If he could get to Anonymous they could attack the system, infiltrate it, plant a spy in the code or take it down. That was a risk they were willing to take. Did they have reason for their confidence or were they just being arrogant? Did they really think a team of second line hackers could handle a full-on assault by the untouchables? Did they have any clue as to whom they'd be up against? The best and the brightest of the web universe had waited since the birth of the internet to take them on. Did they believe they were up against some pimpled group of all-night gamers who'd betray their own for a date with a cheerleader?

He sat there on the soft sofa and calculated probabilities.

He walked over to the center computer and turned it on. Yes, he had access to the net and he tapped it. He googled chess and logged on with the identity: Tekhead3.14. If they wanted a puzzle, let them decipher the meaning of a chess match. In fact, let them deal with a dozen matches. Let them sift through thirty-six simultaneous matches. He took on all challengers, each time adding a numeral to his ID: 3.141, 3.14159, 3.141592 and so forth. The number of pi. Freddie knew that when the number reached the eighteenth digit it would attract attention. He switched over to 3-D imaging and played on. He had moves calculated by pre-arranged algorithms four, five moves in advance. Pawns fell, knights advanced, bishops cut across lanes and castles stood firm. He glided from game to game, making random movements to mislead the monitors, when he saw a flicker of light from a castle and ducked in through the gates. A man holding a candle, dressed as a seventeenth century court jester, beckoned him to follow. He did. They descended a winding stone staircase to an internal chamber of the castle. The man turned and examined him in the dim light.

Who are you?

Who are you?

The image had a flaw in it that made it seem to stammer, pausing between words and speaking staccato.

I am Anonymous.
I'm Freddie Prader.
Where are you?
In the custody of Homeland Security.
Are you sure?

He wasn't. He had assumed as much. Who else had authority to hold a citizen without charge for an indefinite period of time?

No.
Are you on their computer?
Yes.
Thank you.
For what?
You've opened the gate.
Any advice?
Do what you must. Do what you can.

He blew out the candle and Freddie resumed his journey through dozens of chess matches, winning at a ninety percent rate. His mind wandered and he logged off. He felt certain he had made contact with his colleagues at Anonymous. Whether or not his hosts knew it or could eventually decipher it only time would tell.

THE INTERROGATION GAME

Traps
Standing Strong
No Retreat, No Surrender

The interrogations began the moment he arrived at the detention center, a three-hour session in the morning, break for lunch, and another three-hours before dinner. The interrogators tried every tactic in the handbook: good guy, bad guy, confidant, tough love, intimidation, temptation and exasperation. Roy became immune to it all. He recognized the traps, the lies, the exaggerations, the tactics and deceptions. They shot bullets using his writings, bending his words to every purpose. He dodged them and shot back.

Isn't it true that you oppose the American "system of government"?

That's out of context.

What is the correct context?

Read the whole paragraph.

I don't have it.

Then I can't help you.

He opposed the two-party system and its reliance on corporate funding. He opposed the military-industrial complex and the war machine it created. He opposed a government that ignored our most pressing problems, global warming, decaying cities, the ever-increasing divide between the elite and the working class, while it drove the nation into war at every opportunity. He did not oppose democracy. He did not oppose the founding principles and institutions upon which our system of government is based. He opposed those forces that subverted our democracy.

After a couple days he knew they understood. Maybe they even agreed with him but they had a job to do. They wanted a confession. If they could not get a confession, they wanted an admission, contradictory testimony, names or information. They needed the raw materials to construct a web of terrorist conspiracy. Conspiracy is a strange legal concept. Constructed out of wishful thinking to put hardened criminals and racketeers behind bars, it now served the bogeyman known as the War on Terrorism. Evidence of a crime would not be required. The mere suggestion of a crime, the contemplation of a crime would do, even if that contemplation ended in repudiation. In the case of terrorism, the mere suspicions of the arresting body (FBI, Homeland Security, CIA, the Justice Department) were needed with the consent of the White House.

Let's use the word Patriot instead of terrorist. If you talk to a Patriot, does that make you a Patriot? If you discuss patriotic things, possess patriotic symbols, read patriotic books or go to patriotic gatherings, are you then a certified Patriot in the eyes of the law?

Their sessions soon turned into civics lessons that began with his request for an attorney (rejected) and a phone call (rejected) and ended with the interrogator reminding him that he was in very serious trouble. Not only could he be held indefinitely; he could be referred to another nation, a nation that had less restraint.

Nobody out there is trying to help you.

That's a lie.

No one that matters. Where is the famous Roman Mason? Where's Congresswoman Maggie Thomas? Why the silence? And where's Amy?

Running from you.

Why should she run if she has nothing to fear?

She knows patriots and she does patriotic things.

Your friend Freddie has told us everything.

Good. Then I can go.

On and on they went well past the point of absurdity. Like a production of Ionesco's The Bald Soprano, they had no choice but to continue on the circular path their director had charted for them. It occurred to Roy that he really did not know whom the interrogators worked for. Was it the FBI or Homeland Security? Was it someone else? A contractor? He asked them in the manner of their interactions.

If your employer commits a crime, are you also guilty of that crime?

If I knew about it and did nothing, yes.

What if I told you your employer is guilty of a crime? Would you be compelled to do something about it?

Yes.

Tell me who you work for and I'll tell you their crime.

Is this going to be another diatribe on the War Powers Act?

No.

I'm sorry. We're not authorized to divulge...

Well, then, this one's free: They are guilty of imprisoning a free citizen without cause, without evidence and without due process of law.

This interrogator, a woman with a serious demeanor and an obvious grasp not only of the facts but of the affairs of the world, waited, angled her body to block the camera, and whispered: *Damn it, man, why doesn't Representative Thomas speak out!*

A younger man walked into the room with a piece of paper in his hand. Whatever words it contained, the man thought them important enough to interrupt a session, something that did not happen.

What is it?

She read the paper and walked out, the young man following. She returned in five or ten minutes and sat down.

Pardon me. I had to confirm this order. You're free to go.

He stared at her without moving, without emotion, waiting for some explanation or retraction or apology.

You and Freddie Prader are to be released immediately. All charges against Amy Goodall have been dropped. You're free to go.

He followed her out of the interrogation room, read and signed some papers, and reclaimed his belongings. As he walked down the hall to freedom, she grabbed his arm and said: *If you need anyone to testify about what happened here, I'd be happy to oblige.*

She handed him her card and he walked out the doors to a waiting cab.

PERSON OF INTEREST

London Calling
Bloodlines & Money Lines
Eyes, Spies & Lies

John Sinclair had long been a person of interest to the organization that reigned over the world's money supply. He did not possess the bloodline of the elite but his money line ran deep. Sinclair Oil put his family on the map. John had chosen not to walk among them but they followed his career and political accomplishments with interest. The moment he booked flight for London he became a person of interest and the most likely connection that would lead them to Roman Mason.

He booked a room at the St. James, not far from Piccadilly and Charing Cross. He considered it a stylish, comfortable accommodation with all the modern conveniences, an excellent wine selection and fine cuisine, yet lacking the pretentiousness of some of the more traditional luxury hotels. Checking in on a typical sultry summer day, he inquired at the desk about a courier service, instructing the concierge to have someone sent to his room in the next hour. Receiving a generous tip after hauling his luggage to his fourth floor room overlooking the street, the bellboy handed him a small package wrapped in plain brown paper, bowed and walked away.

Sinclair enjoyed puzzles immensely and this one would prove gratifying. Unraveling the wrapping, he found a small rectangular device, about the size of a silver dollar, along with a note: *The item before you is a communication device. It can be used only once and only by the user imprinted in its memory. Keep it on your person at all times. If it vibrates, answer it immediately. If you must contact us, you may do so but only once. If you lose or discard the device, it will be of no use to anyone else. To imprint your identity, open the device and place your right thumb on the window. Do it now.*

Sinclair hesitated and read on.

Remember: Only you can use the device and only you, by pressing your right thumb to the window, can receive messages. Destroy this upon reading. Yours, Anonymous.

He hesitated again while admiring the clever mind or minds behind the invention. Who but Anonymous could come up with such a thing? Who could be trusted if not Freddie's partners in technological resistance? Knowing it could be a mistake, calculating risk and reward, he folded the device open and pressed his thumbprint into the small machine's memory. Lacking an incendiary device, he flushed the note down the toilet and drafted a note to Kenneth Greenwall of The Guardian: *As a friend of Roman Mason, I would like to meet with you regarding matters of immediate importance. If interested, meet me at The Golden Lion around 7 pm. I'll be on the balcony, wearing a distinctive gray Hogan. Yours, John Sinclair.*

Exhausted from the flight, the time change and the disruption to his routine, he waited for the courier, called the desk for a wake-up and a cab, and took a long nap. He dreamed of men in shadows, conspirators hovering above the nameless throng, heartless beings of wealth and status who spoke of common men and women and families as mindless rabble. They called for war and young men marched to their deaths. He saw corpses amidst bombed out rubble, women and children, severed limbs and bloody faces while the moneychangers counted profits. They called for actions against striking workers and clubs bashed heads on picket lines. They called for laws against civil disobedience, civil rights and environmental protection and legislators fell in line. He saw their avarice and greed, their gated castles, their enormous wealth, and their callous disregard of working people and he felt a surging rage rise up from the pit of his soul.

The phone rang, stirring him from deep sleep. He regained his foothold, retraced his footsteps over the last few days, realized he was in a hotel in London and answered the phone. He had just enough time to throw water on his face, tousle his hair, check his pocket for the device, grab his cap and rush downstairs to catch a waiting cab.

He arrived a little late to find a handful of customers mulling about outside. At this hour on a weekday many had already vacated after a long day's labor and a pint for the road home. He admired the black marble columns and the stain glass exterior before ambling inside, ordering a pint of Guinness at the bar and negotiating his way past reveling patrons upstairs to a side seat on the balcony. Lawrence Olivier and his wife Vivian Leigh once inhabited this pub or so he'd been told. Its roots went back three centuries. He sipped his ale and soon found a curious journalist from The Guardian at his table.

Mr. Sinclair?

In person.

Kenneth Greenwall, may I?

He sat looking out at the street, then glancing about, and Sinclair wondered if he thought he'd been followed.

Looking for someone?

You can never be sure.

Indeed.

What can I do for you, Mr. Sinclair?

You can buy me a pint.

From what I hear, you can buy your own.

The man had a sense of humor. Sinclair appreciated his easy manner, his quiet smile, the engaging way he leaned into a conversation. He decided to take it a step further.

I'm interested in securing the freedom of my colleagues in America. I'm told you could be instrumental to that end.

Your colleagues are free.

Really?

It will hit the papers tomorrow. The question remains: Where is the leader, Roman Mason? Rumor has it he is being detained somewhere in Europe.

Interesting rumor. By whom?

That is an excellent question.

I can tell you definitively he is quite free and in Europe. I have reason to believe he is in your fair city as we speak.

Mr. Greenwall contemplated what he had heard as if surprised that Sinclair would reveal as much, as if uncertain that he should possess that information.

Have you contacted him?

I had hoped to but under the circumstances...

You're right to be cautious. You were right to send a courier. I've had a feeling for some time now that my calls have been monitored.

They sipped their ales and watched the lives of Londoners as they moved to and fro on the street below. Sinclair had reached the conclusion that Mr. Greenwall was very probably worthy of trust. Mr. Greenwall had reached a similar conclusion regarding Sinclair.

What can I do for you, Mr. Sinclair?

Should the occasion arise, we'd like to give you an exclusive.

I'd appreciate that.

He finished his ale, rose and tipped his cap.

Be careful.

Always.

Sinclair enjoyed a meal of bangers and mash along with another pint of ale before walking back to the hotel. He had the curious feeling of being followed but he discounted it as alcohol born paranoia. In any case, unless someone meant to rob him on the street, he had nothing to hide at the moment. Back at the hotel, the same man he had met earlier as the bellboy, apparently double shifting as the lift operator, handed him a card advertising a play at the West End Theatre. A note in a small envelope read: *Reserve a ticket for the West End but attend the Royal Court tomorrow eve. Your seat will be reserved under the name Franklin Paine.*

CONTACT

An Evening of Theatre
Patriots and Traitors
Poetic Justice

Here we are: One reserved seat for a Mr. Franklin Paine.
Thank you.

Are you aware your name consists of two famous revolutionaries?

I am: Patriots of the highest magnitude.

To the Americans they're patriots; to the British they're traitors.

Indeed.

It promised to be an interesting evening at the theatre. Having time to spare, he decided a walk to the theatre, allowing a few hours before his arrival, would offer him an opportunity for sightseeing as well as exercise. Within a few blocks he had a vague sense that someone was following him. He tested the hypothesis by garnering the latest issue of The Guardian and lingering on a bench in a courtyard featuring a memorial to the Crimean War. Glancing through Kenneth Greenwall's column entitled "American Independents Set Free" he noted that the article failed to speculate on the whereabouts of founder-leader

Roman Mason. He soon noticed his follower, dressed in typical English youth style, a touch of rebellion with his oversized pants and unlaced boots, short hair cut in a Mohawk, Bob Marley tee under an oversized shirt with short sleeves showing off the tattooed muscles of his biceps, lingering across the street without clear direction or purpose. He moved on and the man followed. Approaching a pub with a gathering of footballers mulling outside, he engaged them and offered to buy the next round if they would detain his pursuer. They looked him over and turned back to Sinclair.

You're not one of those criminal types, are you?

Not by any civilized standard.

Five quid should do.

He handed over a tenner and walked on down the street where he turned to watch the footballers form a semi-circle blocking the man, who made three attempts to maneuver past them before arriving at a logical conclusion and joining them in the pub for a pint.

Sinclair proceeded on a leisurely stroll through the magnificent Buckingham Palace Gardens, a lush forest where bodies of calm water and flashes of brilliant color lay waiting around every corner. He emerged on Buckingham Palace Road where a bustling city life struck a contrast to the pervasive tranquility of the gardens. The palace overrun with tourists and gawkers every one with a camera or rather a phone so equipped. He proceeded to the theatre with ninety minutes to spare, enjoying an early supper of fish and chips at the café below the theatre.

Taking his ticket at the box office, he learned that he had reserved a seat in the last row of the balcony at the upstairs theatre, a smallish venue where young playwrights had an opportunity to produce works on the edge of social acceptability. Tonight's offering by Hayley Squires addressed the pointless endeavor in Afghanistan. When the curtain went up he noted that the seat next to him, the one by the center aisle remained unoccupied. The play pulled him in from its opening moments, its characters coming alive and seizing his empathy while a sense of the inevitable ripped at his heart. He didn't notice that a strange man with a full beard, a cap and coat more suitable to fishing than to the theatre, sat in the chair beside him under the cover of darkness. He decided he should be a little annoyed until he realized, just short of first intermission, that it had to be Roman Mason.

Engaging, isn't it.

The play or the costuming?

Both. Sadly, we will be unable to attend the second act.

Shameful.

I've explained to the proprietor we have a pressing engagement. We'll be chunneling to the continent.

They boarded a high-speed train at St. Pancras International Station and in the approximate time it takes to experience a play in London they emerged on the fertile ground of France. In a little over two hours they arrived at Gare du Nord Station in Paris. In the interim they discussed what had transpired and plotted their future course of action. Still on the train, they used their one call to Anonymous.

How was the Chunnel?

Exhilarating.

Rome explained that he would be contacting Prince Georg to accept the Overlords' invitation on the condition that Sinclair should be included as a full partner. They expected the condition to be granted.

A PATRIOT DIRGE

Within twenty-four hours they expected to be flown on a private plane to one of the elite castles in their realm for an induction ceremony. Because of its splendor and isolation, Rome believed it would be Ksiaz Castle in Poland while Sinclair believed it would be the island castle of Mont Saint Michel on the northwest coast of France for similar reasons. But no one outside the elite circle could be certain. They had independently arrived at the conclusion that the Overlords would be in attendance but not in the ceremonial hall. Rather, they would monitor the ceremony from a smaller chamber above the hall, like a king would observe his courtesans.

We're on it.

You'd better be. We're not likely to get a second chance.

At some level you just have to have faith.

Translation: It is best not to say too much even on an encrypted line.

Should we discard this device?

Not until necessary. You can still receive messages and it is of no value to anyone else.

They managed to book a room with a view at the Hotel Notre Dame in the heart of Paris. Sinclair tapped his Paris connection and paid an exorbitant fee. The view of the Seine and the cathedral at night inspired dreams of all that humankind can achieve. The island from which Notre Dame rises is the birthplace of this grand European metropolis, dating back before Christ walked the earth. It seemed a fitting place for two master chess players to plan their final moves.

Rome made the call.

Mr. Mason! You have been quite the mystery man.

As I said, I needed seven days.

Yes, but we did not expect you to vanish from the earth.

I assure you, I have not left the planet.

Where are you now?

Rome laid his cards on the table. There would be no more deceptions, no more hiding and no more subterfuge.

I am in Paris at the Hotel Notre Dame.

Have you considered our proposal?

I have. I am prepared to accept on three conditions: First, that no harm should come to my former colleagues or their loved ones by your hands. Second, that you will not impede their work. Third, that you will also accept my partner in this venture, a man I believe you may be familiar with, a Mr. John Sinclair.

Mr. Sinclair?

Yes.

He may or may not have been surprised but his voice signaled that he was. In fact, he had met Sinclair on any number of occasions but did not say so.

I'm certain that your terms are reasonable but naturally I must consult with my colleague before rendering a decision. A little patience, Mr. Mason, I will call you back.

They took a long walk along the Seine, the golden light of the city shimmering on its rippled surface, speaking of all things political and aesthetic, the grandeur of an ancient metropolis, the inspiration of her art and architecture, her fabled history of kings, emperors and revolutionaries, its brilliant philosophers and its embrace of artists. No place on earth rivaled Paris in the elegance of its achievements and perhaps no place had suffered as much from its shortcomings.

They dined on the Avenue of le Grande Armee, gazing at the Arch de Triumph, commemorating France's liberation from Nazi occupation, and drank wine late into the night under a starlit sky of a million dreams. There was little more they could do but wait and think and consider all possibilities. Soon everything would change. Whether it changed only for them or for the entire world and its posterity depended on how it played out.

A toast to the man without a country:

We have it in our power to begin the world over again!

ANONYMOUS RISING

Out of the Shadows
A Cause and an Action
A Voice for the Voiceless

"We are Anonymous. We are Legion. We do not forgive. We do not forget."

Out of the shadows they emerged with the power of knowledge, righteousness and anonymity. The power of anonymity cannot be understated. You cannot seek vengeance on the unknown. You cannot threaten or punish those you cannot see. You cannot prosecute, imprison or detain a sliver of light in the darkness.

Born of the internet in 2003, its cardinal mission to protect the worldwide web from the corporate and governmental powers that wish to control it, its disparate members seek justice for the powerless and provide a voice for the voiceless.

When an all-powerful, all-knowing organization without a name, itself shielded by the veil of anonymity, went after Freddie Prader, they declared war on Anonymous. When they detained him without due process, they invited the wrath of a snake with a thousand heads. They would learn. They would pay a price.

Those who characterize Anonymous as a single

entity know nothing of the organization. It is not a thing that can be defined and contained. It is infinity squared. Bound by a concept of justice and a moral code upholding the dignity of humankind, its members are free to choose a cause and an action according to their own interests. The cause of Freddie Prader attracted the best and the brightest of Anonymous.

They pooled their resources, their knowledge and abilities, and determined a course of action that would not only free Freddie but also extract a price to ensure that never again would any organization act with such callous regard for individual rights.

They reached out across the globe and mobilized for the assault. This time it would not be as simple as hacking a system or a central computer. This time it required boots on the ground, armed with the latest and greatest surveillance technology the world's most brilliant technological minds could produce. They raised an army of Anonymous soldiers that converged on the castles of Europe.

Among the arsenal in their repertoire of weaponry: virtually silent miniature drones with night vision to survey the target structure and its surroundings, microphones that could record whispers through windows and curtains in great clarity at a distance exceeding 500 yards and cameras that could record images in high definition by bouncing off reflective surfaces (mirrors, glass, strips of metal) at an even greater distance.

But their key weapon, an Anonymous invention, one that no one to their knowledge had ever developed or deployed, was a tiny electronic robot that could form itself into a ball, be shot out of an air gun or dropped from a miniature drone, and remotely guided to a target position. It could climb walls, negotiate stairs, creep under doors and attach itself to virtually any surface: light fixtures and chandeliers, a picture frame or the corner of a room.

Once attached at a suitable location, it could record all images and sounds within a confined space. Its key limitation was that it could be detected by the naked eye and by an electronic sweep. Their adversaries in this mission would be sure to sweep any room that the Overlords would inhabit. Therefore, the device could not be put in place until after the sweep had taken place.

They had taken all precautions. Every squad at each of the castles deemed most likely for their isolation and design had at least one local familiar with the environment. Every member had been thoroughly vetted. With the latest information, reinforcements had been sent to Ksiaz Castle and Mont Saint Michel.

The shallow waters of the Gulf of Saint Malo protected Saint Michel. Dating back to the sixth century, the island castle contains a temple at its top, an abbey and a monastery above its grand reception halls with a village of commoners at its base. Still inhabited, its population is a meager 44 citizens. A spectacular vision, springing from the calm waters of the bay to the heavens, it welcomed millions of visitors every year. It seemed both secure (any boat attempting to monitor its activities would certainly be detected) and able to accommodate a large party with half a dozen hotels in the immediate surroundings.

Of the two Ksiaz, located on a mountaintop in a dense forest, was the most isolated although it did have an adjoining hotel. The hotel made it both less and more likely to be selected:

It provided accommodations that a large wealthy party might require but also gave possible access to outsiders. They monitored reservations and had discovered that reservations were not available on the night in question. Maybe it had already been booked or maybe a wealthy and powerful party had asserted its authority. They made inquiries and found that, indeed, those who had long-standing reservations suddenly received notices of cancellation.

While Ksiaz seemed probable they would not put all their money on one stock. The enemy might be smarter than anticipated. The block of reservations might be a decoy. They reinforced their encampment in the forest below Ksiaz but they did not pull out of Saint Michel or any other base of operations. They stayed silent, out of sight and waited. The target area had been identified. The plan of attack had been finalized. They knew where to drop the surveillance robots. They knew where to guide them and what to avoid.

As night gave way to day and day to night they observed guests leaving the hotel but none arriving. They witnessed a flurry of activity inside the castle. The staff hustled to make ready for a last minute event and one of great importance. They observed a target laid out on the grass courtyard dividing the castle from the hotel. The dignitaries would arrive by limousine, the Overlords by helicopter.

They hunkered down as a security chopper flew low over the forest circling the castle looking for any signs of human presence. They found none. The saw nothing but trees and brush, maybe a pack of wild boar, elk, lynx and an occasional wolf. Humans did not inhabit this forest of protected land and they saw no signs of them.

The time was upon them and like a predator perched over his pray, without breath or motion, the army of the unknown stood ready to strike.

THE CEREMONY

Conditions Accepted
Meeting the Masters
The Greater Good

A knock on the door of their room at the Notre Dame Hotel at about half past three in the afternoon signaled the deliverance of their invitations to a grand celebration. The timing suggested an estimated arrival time between seven and eight at Castle Ksiaz in Poland. Sinclair smiled and handed Rome a silver dollar.

The courier presented a handwritten note to Rome and a card for each of them. The note said: Conditions accepted. Embossed in gold lettering reading "The House of Hapsburg-Lorraine" around the edges, the cards read:

Please accept this invitation to a celebration of your achievement in ascending to a position of eminent esteem.

Longer than the message, the signature removed all doubt as to the location of the induction ceremony:

The Honorable Karl von Hapsburg, Prince Imperial & Archduke of Austria, Prince Royal of Hungary & Bohemia, House of Hapsburg-Lorraine, Order of the Golden Fleece.

One of the oldest of the royal families of Europe, Hapsburg dated back to the thirteenth century, reaching its peak with Maximilian the First and Charles the Fifth as Emperors of the Holy Roman Empire. The bloodline produced numerous kings and queens from Austria, Hungary, Germany and Bohemia to France and Spain, including the ill-fated Marie Antoinette. The Hapsburg Dynasty unofficially ended in 1918 with the virtual abdication of Charles the First. The official end of the dynasty came in 1961 when the eldest son of Charles, Otto von Hapsburg, renounced all claims to the Austrian throne. The eldest son of Otto, Karl von Hapsburg inherited the titles stripped of entitlement.

None of this meant a great deal to Rome or Sinclair. They did not consider the heir to the defunct dynasty a member of the elite but it amused them that the Overlords seemed to collect royalty as pawns or rather knights and bishops on their side of the board. The Overlords would never allow their names or faces to be identified with an official gathering or event. They hovered above the proceedings where cameras and microphones could not reach or at least so they believed.

Driven to the airport, they boarded a private plane and departed knowing their anonymous friends would follow their position. In what might be considered a breach of security, they would not insist that Sinclair discard his communication device until they entered the castle. They dressed aboard the plane, tuxedos and tails, and completed their journey on a private helicopter.

Meantime, hiding in the forest about the castle, anonymous foot soldiers observed the arrival of thirty-six guests in a series of limousines and twelve dignitaries in helicopters before the guests of honor arrived. They observed carefully the activities in

Maximillian Hall, where the celebration would be held, and above in the King's Chamber, where the Overlords would assemble. A surge in electromagnetic radiation informed them when the security sweep had been completed. They launched two mini-drones, guiding them to the drop zone with the precision of a skilled surgeon's scalpel. The drop successful, they remotely guided two teams of four tiny mobile robots, one on a course to the King's Chamber and the other to Maximillian Hall below, each staggered in its progress so that any mishap with one would not endanger the others. If one was discovered they could disarm it. It would appear as a curious metal ball, perhaps a child's toy, and would not alarm security unless closely inspected.

The robots entered the castle through a ventilation shaft and, holding tight to the walls, progressed through a servant station to a hallway, down a flight of stairs, where the first team split off down another hallway to the chamber door. The second team proceeded down another flight of stairs to Maximillian Hall. One by one the first team crept by an unsuspecting guard, under the door and climbed the walls, implanting themselves one in each corner of the exquisitely furnished room, a room made fit for a king or an emperor with rare classical art and the brilliant crimson and gold emblem of the Hapsburg Dynasty. The golden lion reigned over all that transpired here. Twelve men in expensive tailored suits gathered in groups of two and three, sitting on velvet sofas and chairs, sipping drinks of choice and chattering on diverse subjects. They all but ignored three large television screens displaying the events in the grand gathering hall below.

The second team of miniatures implanted themselves in each corner of the expansive Maximillian Hall. Every square inch of the hall with its magnificent mirrors, its golden chandeliers, its ceiling fresco of Mount Parnassus, its Baroque décor, along with every inhabitant of the hall and the chamber above was now under surveillance.

A quick sound and visual check and they went live on the worldwide web. No titles, no names and no explanation, the initial pod cast went out to three internal websites where facial recognition software was applied. Minute by minute, the hits came up, the players were identified, but it would remain in house until the on-sight team gave the signal to disseminate.

Rome and Sinclair entered the grand reception hall to the standing ovation of all in attendance. Rome recognized some of their smiling, inebriated faces from his first encounter at Hohenzollern Castle only a week ago. Prince George greeted them with a personal handshake and escorted them to their seats next to Prince von Hapsburg who stood at the head of the table. At the gentle clang of a crystal wine glass, the guests sat and the prince began the ceremony.

We are gathered here to celebrate the induction of not one but two new members to our esteemed fraternity. It is rare indeed that two men should be welcomed to the fold on one occasion but these two men have taken a unique path to this accomplishment. The first might have taken this honor years, dare I say, decades ago but he did not fully appreciate the virtue of our enterprise at that time. We are always pleased when time resolves our petty conflicts to bring us together. He is a man of inherited wealth who put those resources to good use in causes to improve the lot of humankind. Some say he is the mastermind behind the unprecedented success of the American Independent Movement. I give you Mr. John Sinclair, Esquire.

The guests followed their leader in applause and all eyes turned to Sinclair who had not prepared any particular remarks. Upstairs the Overlords observed the proceedings as fans might observe a football match, with a running commentary on the performance. One remarked that Prince Karl still believed that one day he would be returned to the throne, King Karl of Austria, Hungary and Bohemia, Emperor of the Seven Kingdoms, Lord Protector of Jerusalem and Holy Sovereign of all he beholds. Sinclair spoke and the Overlords became attentive, more curious than intrigued.

One cannot escape or alter one's familial upbringing or legacy. One can only accept the gifts and opportunities one is given and act according to one's conscience. That I have done so is what I hope shall distinguish my life. In that regard, I am humbled and grateful for the opportunity your organization has afforded me.

He raised his glass to toast the Golden Fleece and "all that it signifies". The guests dutifully raised their glasses and drank though some could be heard wondering in whispers what indeed the toast meant. Upstairs in the King's Chamber they enjoyed the novelty of an unpredictable member. More than any other single factor, they sought Rome Mason to shake things up. They had far too many members who went along, who followed directives, who never thought or spoke out of turn. These ceremonies had become as predictable as the salivation of Pavlov's dogs. Now it seemed John Sinclair would also add to the flavor of their proceedings.

Thank you, Mr. Sinclair, for a very eloquent acceptance.

Our second inductee and singular guest of honor is a man who exemplifies the American dream, who pulled himself up by his proverbial bootstraps, succeeded magnificently as an entrepreneur, and transferred that genius to electoral politics. He stood up to the awesome power of the American government not once but twice.

The guests chuckled and the Overlords above laughed aloud.

He is the founder and leader of the American Independent Movement, the man who could be president or rather might have been, Mr. Roman Mason.

Rome stood with a smile as genuine as he could affect. He felt the eyes and ears of the Overlords upon him, the men who determined the course of history, as they had for a thousand years. Perhaps more. He felt the weight of all that history, of kings and queens and despots and dictators and corporate masters and hereditary succession and bankers and wealth and corruption, press down upon his shoulders.

Ever since I could stand on my own two feet, ever since I could think for myself, my sole motivation has been the greater good. When I engaged the business world and accumulated wealth it was not for myself; it was for the greater good. As I looked back upon my life one week ago today, I could take some satisfaction that the world is better off for my having been. But it is not enough. As we all know, the greatest threat we face today is the warming of the planet by our own hands. As we all know, what we have done to hold back this grave threat, at a cost of countless species and millions of human lives, is inadequate.

As I reflected on these circumstances, I ultimately had no choice but to seize the moment, to grasp this opportunity for the greater good. And so I thank you for extending your hand to welcome my partner and me. We thank you for providing this opportunity to engage this critical enterprise. If we can make California a model of green energy, if we can prove to the world that ending our dependence on fossil fuels is not only possible and sustainable but also economical and profitable, we can change the world. A week ago today, Prince George presented his proposal, his invitation to join your circle, to gain a seat at the table, and asked: Isn't that what you've always wanted? After a week's reflection and soul-searching, I would have to answer No. What I've always wanted is to change the world. But at this time and place in history, this is the best we can do: The greater good.

He raised his glass to toast and triggered the ritual of the royal houses. Prince Karl stood and pronounced, "Here, here! To the House of Hapsburg!" Around the table they went: The House of Lorraine, the House of Bourbon, the House of Stuart, on and on. When it at last came to Sinclair, he toasted the House of Spirits and Rome saluted the House of the Rising Sun. "Here, here!"

The ceremony completed, they enjoyed an exquisite five-course meal and the spirits flowed freely. Upstairs, the Overlords enjoyed their own exquisite meal, exchanging knowing smiles and lively discussion. For the second time in many years, they found the entertainment engaging and satisfying. Those who had pushed for Roman Mason's invitation and the acceptance of Sinclair as an equal partner felt vindicated. Those who stood in opposition to both measures held on to their doubts: Sure, they were engaging and entertaining but could they be trusted?

If either or both present a problem, we do what we do best.

Eliminate the problem.

Of course, but such matters can be messy.

Remember that reporter who flew too close to the sun?

Mr. Hastings?

Yes. Whatever the suspicions it could never be traced back to us.

A groundbreaking journalist, whose investigative report on General Stanley McChrystal, commander of American forces in Afghanistan, forced the commander's resignation, Michael Hastings died in a single car accident in Los Angeles. Despite highly suspicious circumstances and speculation that Hastings was about to break a huge story regarding NSA surveillance of American citizens, the LAPD classified his death as an accident, perhaps a suicide. His friends and colleagues took issue with that conclusion but the case had been sealed and all efforts to examine the vehicle and the remains had been blocked.

As the guests consumed desert, the Overlords sent a messenger to summon the new recruits for a meeting in the King's Chamber. They entered the double doors of the chamber to find twelve men seated in a semi-circle at a round table. The lighting had been lowered and arranged to backlight the Overlords so that their honored guests could not see or observe their faces. One of the darkened faces spoke.

We thought you might want to use this opportunity to make inquiries of those who will serve as your superiors in this enterprise.

Rome looked to Sinclair. They had discussed this possibility but concluded it was unlikely at this juncture of their relationship. They nevertheless hoped for the opportunity and prepared accordingly.

Indeed. We should like to know who you are.

What is your organizational structure?

Voices in the darkness emerged from different

sources yet one mind, making it difficult to discern for a moment where the voice came from.

We owe our legacy to the aristocracy as you might have surmised. For a thousand years we reigned over the western world by way of the royal houses of Europe. With colonization we expanded to the Americas and parts of Asia.

We bow to no Kings, no Queens, no presidents, no prime ministers, no military commanders or corporate entities.

Indeed, they bow to us.

For the last century we have ruled the world not as an aristocracy but a meritocracy. We twelve once stood where you stand today. Therefore, you may aspire to one day fill our seats.

They had not expected the Overlords to be forthcoming but why wouldn't they be? They possessed absolute certainty that whatever occurred in this chamber would remain here. It spoke of an arrogance that came with omnipotent power. Rome pressed them.

What is the source of your power?

Quite simply, we control the world's essential resources. Minerals, plutonium, uranium, fossil fuels, potable water, dams, electrical grids, virtually everything that is required to keep a modern civilization running. We control technology and we control the sun. We do not fear a green economy for we will control it.

How do you maintain control?

By any and all means. In the modern world, information is power. With rare exceptions, information is all we require to enforce our policies and eliminate problems.

What happens if we reject your authority? If we decide at some future time to return to our independent lives, what consequences might we expect to face?

A rumbling of quiet discontent emerged from the

darkness, as if those who opposed the inclusion of Rome Mason and John Sinclair asserted their concern. The voice that spoke next reverberated strength and decisiveness.

Perhaps we should have been more explicit. Once you walked into these doors any possibility of changing your minds disintegrated.

Nevertheless...

You would become a problem and we would be forced to do what we do best: Eliminate problems. Are we being clear?

I believe so but just to be certain: If we became a problem, you would eliminate us.

A voice from the ensuing silence said yes and then another and another. Rome and Sinclair felt like chastised children. No longer would they be allowed to play with the other children's toys. Already they had managed to betray the trust.

We do not anticipate having to take drastic actions. In fact, we have not been compelled to do so in some fifty years.

1963.

A beeping sound could just be detected in the background of the chamber. One by one the Overlords took notice until chaos reined over their proceeding.

Can someone tell me what the hell that is?

Rome and Sinclair knew the answer and in a gesture of generosity they decided to share their secret knowledge with the masters of secret knowledge.

It seems clear to me, gentlemen, that you are being monitored.

A team of security agents burst through the door and began scanning for surveillance devices. One by one the mini-robots dropped from their corner positions and scattered, delaying the moment of their detection. Sinclair bowed.

We sirs shall take our leave.

The hell you will!

Are you holding us against our will?

If this is what I think it is, holding you is the least of your worries!

That sounds like a threat.

Take them away.

Before two guards could enforce the order, shots rang out in the distance, sounding unreal, like a construction crew three blocks down: bap-bap, bap! Three shots, silence, and then a scream. Not a movie scream, not a loud, high-pitched emission calculated to stun, but an involuntary expression of horror and disbelief.

They shot a man on public land, in a forest thick with brush and trees. They could not have seen what or at whom they were shooting. They heard something, saw a flicker of light, and fired indiscriminately.

What have you done? challenged Rome. *Call off your dogs!*

A guard rushed in to report what had happened. A man had been shot, the rest captured. They could find no recording device. Rome felt the rage of injustice rise in his soul and wanted to strangle the man before him.

Damn you to hell! Did you really think you could control the worldwide web? If you google Overlords at this very moment you will discover the error born of your arrogance.

One of them did so and within moments they witnessed the awesome power of Anonymous: There on three large-screen televisions they observed their own proceedings and those of their underlings in the grand hall below. The setting, the event and every individual was identified, with their biographies, business connections, philanthropic endeavors, personal and family histories accessible at the click of a mouse.

They watched in rapt silence as the importance of what they were seeing resonated within each of their souls. Their world had changed.

Let them go. We have far more important matters before us.

It was all Sinclair could do not to retort: *No, you do not. That is the point.*

The world had changed.

THE MEN WHO CONTROLLED THE WORLD

The Power of Transparency
Democracy's Second Chance
The New World Order

Kenneth Greenwall's column read in part:

Mark your calendars. Yesterday a pod cast went out on the worldwide web that has the power to alter the very nature of the world as we know it. Appearing under the title "The Overlords: Twelve Men who Rule the World" it reveals the identity of an elite organization that claims to have possessed such power for a thousand years. The pod cast's authenticity has been verified by multiple sources and investigations of the group's activities are currently under way. When an organization no matter how omnipotent depends on anonymity for its power and when that anonymity is replaced by transparency, its power ceases to exist.

The great mystery now is what will fill the power void. We do not know if there exists a court large enough, broad enough and courageous enough to bring these men to justice for crimes against humanity. We know that the statute of limitations has long elapsed for the greatest of their crimes. We know that our history is filled with monarchs, dictators and presidents who have committed crimes against humanity with impunity. Perhaps the best we can hope for is that these men and their organization will simply cease to do harm. If we apply the light of public scrutiny and relentlessly pursue them as the paparazzi pursue Jay Z and Beyonce or the latest royal couple, then their thousand-year reign must come to its final end.

We know that all of the nations that bowed to their power have governments and most of those nations are representative democracies. We can only hope that in the light of this knowledge, the electorates of those democracies will finally assert themselves. In the coming weeks the intricate web of connections from the Overlords to our elected officials will be revealed. No power on earth can suppress this information. Do not be surprised if this disease infects most of our officials, our diplomats and ministers. It will then fall to us, the electorate, to clear out the corrupt and replace them with a clean slate.

Beware those so-called journalists who will tell you, day after day, week after week, that this is not an important story, the puff and stuff of conspiracy theorists. They are either the victims of a centuries old propaganda campaign or they are themselves corrupt. This is the most important story in a thousand years.

While those of us who have investigated widespread government corruption, those of us who have wondered at how an elected government could so consistently represent such a small, elite portion of the electorate, those of us who have speculated at the existence of an elite organization with disproportionate influence, now have cause for vindication, even celebration, we must acknowledge that this story did not come without a price.

A young man who participated in the surveillance

operation, a member of the loose collaboration of internet wizards known as Anonymous, paid for this story with his life. Huddled with his friends and their high tech equipment in the woods below Ksiaz Castle in Poland, where the elite gathered, their presence was detected and the guards charged with protecting the gathering fired indiscriminately into the forest. One of their bullets found the head of young Daniel Volcek, an internet consultant from the Czech Republic. Their intention, we are told, was to capture the intruders and confiscate their recordings. Little did they know there were no recordings to be confiscated. The images and sound went out live on the worldwide web.

Daniel died a hero and a patriot of the highest order. He played his part in what could become a global Velvet Revolution and it claimed his life.

We cannot know how this will end but we do know this: At this late date, democracy has a second chance. In the words of Pete Townshend, we should "get down on our knees and pray we won't get fooled again."

Sinclair and Mason read Greenwall's words with a deep sense of gratification. After they took Daniel to the nearest hospital where he was pronounced dead, they caught a ride from their anonymous friends, rode to the nearest airport and booked the next flight to Paris. They desperately needed to leave Polish soil behind, as if the entire country had been contaminated by what had transpired there. They did not breathe until they landed at Charles De Gaulle airport. There they picked up a copy of The Guardian, stopped at the first outdoor café they came across and read his words. At least someone understood. At least someone fully appreciated what they had done and why they had done it.

They had passed on an opportunity to do a great good for the chance of achieving a greater good. They could not know how it would turn out. They took a leap of faith. They trusted their gut feelings. They seized the moment.

Back in Paris, under a brilliant starlit Parisian sky, they understood what so many Parisians had historically felt: the need to act, the need for fundamental change, a need so basic they would risk everything. They belonged with the people, not the elite. They had rejected the sainted halls of the overlords and joined the Paris Communard. The communards of 1871 had stood together in a line, backs against the wall at Pere LaChaise cemetery 147 strong, were shot down and buried in a common grave. The communards sacrificed everything for the cause. Unlike the Communard, Rome and Sinclair and the Independent Movement had not only survived but prevailed.

They called their colleagues and loved ones back in the states to relate what had happened. Everyone already knew. More details had been revealed. More names had come out along with their relations, financial and otherwise, to prominent world leaders. The people filled the streets and city squares in mass protest once again. Everywhere the people chanted Rome's name and called for him to run for president. Voters stood in long lines to register with the American Independent Movement. Thousands applied to attend the national convention. Tens of thousands converged on Seattle. Working people from Portland, Maine to Portland, Oregon and everywhere in between, wrote checks and volunteered time. Far from crippled, the

Independent Movement thrived.

They postponed their return to America to attend the funeral of Daniel Volcek in Prague. Amazed at how quickly the word spread, they joined thousands upon thousands who converged from all over the world on that ancient city of enlightenment to pay tribute and mourn. They knew then that this story would not die as Daniel had. He had not died in vain.

They returned to America celebrated as heroes. Even the rightwing reactionaries were afraid to attack them openly. Everything had changed.

Maggie pleaded with Rome to accept the nomination to run for president. Knowing he had no desire to run and less to serve in any public office, the rising tide of support nevertheless provided an opportunity that no one could fulfill but him. "For the greater good," she said. He could only consider the possibility. Things change. Everything changes. Meantime, it seemed he and Sinclair would be able to attend the convention after all. He wanted to address the delegates. He had a few observations and reflections he wished to share.

Sinclair, sitting in the airport lounge, awaiting their flight home, could only smile. He remained behind the curtains as he always had. In the proper execution of his duties, the operative receives little credit when a campaign succeeds and much blame when it fails. Destiny decreed that he and his like would witness history from the sideline. He had been cast as Sancho Panza to Rome's Don Quixote.

On the day of the convention, Rome watched the proceedings from his apartment. He would be the keynote speaker. The streets were filled with activists, summoning his name and crying out for justice. Inside the hall, the energy soared with a sense of hope and optimism he had never seen in his life. As the moment approached, he took a cab and crawled through traffic as far as he could and then got out and walked. The crowd so thick he could hardly move until someone recognized him and called out to the rest: *This is Rome Mason! Clear the way!*

"Rome 4 President!" signs were everywhere along with the usual assortment of issue oriented messages. A collection of men and women formed a circle around him and guided him forward to the convention center. They entered the auditorium and marched down the center aisle and delegates erupted in applause as he passed. He raised his hands in a plea for silence as a tribute to Daniel Volcek played on the screen behind the speaker's podium – a documentary entitled A Patriot Dirge.

He waited until the presentation was over and waited again before taking the stage. As the applause at length subsided he said: *It has not been my good fortune to have a son in this life but if I had I would have wanted a son like Daniel Volcek.*

A few cries of affirmation surrendered to a rolling wave: *We want Rome! We want Rome! We want Rome!*

He cleared his throat, wiped his eyes and began his remarks with the words of a man without a country:

"We ought to reflect, that there are three different ways by which independence may hereafter be effected, and that one of those three, will, one day or other, be the fate of America: By the legal voice of the people in Congress; by a military power, or by a mob. It may not always happen that our soldiers are citizens, and the multitude a body of reasonable men. Virtue is not hereditary and neither is it perpetual. Should independence be brought about by the first

of those means, we have every opportunity and every encouragement before us, to form the noblest, purest republic on the face of the earth. We have it in our power to begin the world over again. A situation, similar to the present, hath not happened since the days of Noah until now.

"The birthday of a new world is at hand, and humankind is about to receive their portion of freedom from the events of a few months. The reflection is awesome and in this point of view, how trifling, how ridiculous, do the little paltry cavilings of a few weak or interested men appear, when weighed against the business of a world."

Those words from Common Sense written by Thomas Paine, the founder too often forgotten in the annals of history, ring as true today as they did in 1776.

"We have it in our power to begin the world over again." Now as then, we must not fail. For the sake of the planet and all who live within her realm, we must not fail.

The crowd roared and the waves of support swept through him: *We want Rome! We want Rome!*

He listened intently, he felt their collective heartbeat, he absorbed their hopes and dreams and he thought: *Can I do this?* He listened and he thought:

Yes, I can.

ABOUT THE AUTHOR

His roots firmly planted in the fertile central valley of California, Jack Random has lived a rich and varied life from the university square to the streets of Manhattan, from the adventures of a hitchhiker to the classrooms of public schools. He has been an actor, a poet, a playwright and a writer of fiction, a political essayist, a teacher, a student and a seeker of truth.

He is the author of *Wasichu: The Killing Spirit, Number Nine: The Adventures of Jake Jones and Ruby Daulton,* the *Jazzman Chronicles: Volumes I-X* (Crow Dog Press) and *Ghost Dance Insurrection* (Dry Bones Press).

www.ingramcontent.com/pod-product-compliance
Lightning Source LLC
Chambersburg PA
CBHW032210190626
46810CB00019B/2427

* 9 7 8 0 6 9 2 5 4 8 1 9 6 *